READ

Heat

Also by Geneva Holliday

Groove

Fever

WRITING AS BERNICE L. McFADDEN

Sugar

The Warmest December

This Bitter Earth

Loving Donovan

Camilla's Roses

Nowhere Is a Place

Heat

Geneva Holliday

BROADWAY BOOKS

New York

For my soul mate:
I'm here, I'm ready, I'm waiting . . .

Heat

This, that, and the third . . .

March

Crystal

. . . .

I'm sick of making breakfast for my vibrator!"

I screamed into the phone to Noah, who was laughing his ass off in his flat in London.

"Stop laughing, Noah. It's not funny."

"I know, I'm sorry, baby. I wish I could help you out, but you know I've been off the coochie for some time now." He snickered.

"Whatever," I said through a yawn.

"I gotta go, babe. We'll talk again next week, okay?"

"Okay."

"Love you."

"Love you too," I said, and hung up the phone. Stretching myself out onto my couch, I began to evaluate my situation.

Maybe the fact that it's been a long time since I've had a real live man in my bed is what has put me in such a funky mood to begin with.

Maybe it's not just the absence of sex—maybe I'm depressed?

I've thought about that. Even ventured so far as to speak to a couple of associates who make it no secret that they pop Xanax as often as Geneva pops M&M's.

They tell me I don't have the symptoms of depression. They say, "Maybe you're just dissatisfied with your life?"

How could I be?

I'm a director at a very successful nonprofit organization. I pull in a six-figure income, I own a beautiful apartment overlooking Central Park, and I have a very hefty 401(k). And let's not forget good health, friends, and family.

I have everything a girl could want—except a man. Well, I sort of have a man—well, a part-time lover really . . . in Antigua no less.

But I want . . . I need my very own man.

Up until this moment I haven't wanted to admit that to myself, but true is true and sometimes the truth is a hard fact to face. I guess I didn't want to own up to it because I didn't want to fall into the category of "Only Feels Complete with a Man."

I think this Strong Black Woman complex hurts a lot of us strong black women. We're supposed to be these alpha females with power jobs that allow us to buy ourselves our own power toys.

Have you noticed the number of women who own cars now?

And I read that black women own more real estate than black men.

Those women, the strong black ones, proclaim that they don't need a man for anything, don't even need their dicks. Those they can buy online in any size, shape, and color.

I should know: I have two dildos and a vibrator shaped like a ladybug.

I may seem like one of those women—the strong black women—my trappings may suggest that I am, but truth be told, I'm not.

I may not be verbalizing that I need a man, but shit, in my heart I'm screaming that I do.

A dildo can't hold you, embrace you after sex, or take you on romantic walks along moon-kissed beaches. It can't propose marriage, and, worst of all, it can't give you children.

So if not wanting any of those things, or not needing any of those things, is what makes a strong black woman, then a strong black woman I'm not.

Over the past year I've put my heart into finding that special someone. I did the speed-dating thing and just walked away with a dry mouth and stiff jaws from smiling too much. I even went the online route and actually thought I'd stumbled onto a "possible" when I met Ben.

Benjamin Knight was a tall brown-skinned man with curly sandy-colored hair and hazel eyes. A pharmacist by trade, he had great teeth and a nice physique.

He had twin boys named Clarence and Fabian and an ex-wife named Nadia.

Ben had given Nadia the house in Westchester County and rented a small apartment for himself in Greenwich Village. He'd always wanted to live in the Village, he confided to me on our first date as we sat sipping wine at the Harlem Grill. "I've got an artist's heart," he'd said, laughing.

I liked his laugh.

"So what are you looking for in a mate?" The question was sudden, totally taking me off guard.

"Well, I um . . ." I started, not knowing how we'd gotten to that place so quickly. I glanced down at my watch. We were just thirty minutes in. "I guess I want what all women want," I said, hoping that I would not have to say any more than that.

Ben nodded his head. He understood, or at least I thought he did. I would find out a week later that what he thought all women wanted and what I wanted were two very different things.

After the lovely meal and lively conversation, he drove me home in his brand-new emerald green Jaguar. Walking me to the front door of my building, he placed both of his hands on my shoulders, leaned in, and gave me a polite peck on my forehead. Afterward, he reiterated what a wonderful time he'd had and how he hoped I wouldn't break his heart by telling him that I already had plans for next Friday night.

I didn't.

We spoke twice during the week. He was funny, insightful, and intelligent. I was beginning to think that I'd finally hit the jackpot. But when he called Thursday evening to confirm the time and place for our second date, the jackpot I thought I'd hit turned into just the two-dollar winnings on a quarter bet.

"Hey, Crystal, I was wondering . . . maybe we can, uh, skip the dinner," he said.

"Okay, is there something else you'd like to do instead?" I asked as I stood over my dressing table, unhooking my watch from my wrist.

"Yeah, I figure you can just come over to my place or I can hang out at yours."

The red flag started to inch up the flagpole, but I ignored it.

He was cute, smart, a good and attentive father. His ex-wife didn't work; she didn't have to, and besides, he didn't want her to. It was important, he said, for his children not to have to be raised by nannies and babysitters.

So he's paying a mortgage, child and spousal support, not counting his expenses—maybe his request to stay in came from a financial aspect?

The excuses swirled around me.

"Um, well—" I began.

"Look, Crystal. We're both adults, so we know where we're going to end up, and I—"

" 'End up'?"

"Yeah, end up."

"Where's that?"

"In bed. I want you, you want me, so why do we have to play these stupid games? Dinner, movies. All of it a waste of money and time. We could be using that time getting to know each other. You know, in the biblical sense."

I was flabbergasted. "Are you joking?"

"No."

Click.

That was the end of Ben.

Then there was Sultan.

I know—what kind of name is that?

Well, I thought it was the one his mama gave him. His government name, as they say.

But come to find out, it was the name he gave himself in prison while he was serving a six-to-ten stint. Of course, I didn't find out that he'd been in prison until our fourth date, when we ended up in my apartment, in my bedroom.

I was wet as hell; I mean, the fucking Niagara was spilling out from between my legs. At that point I hadn't had sex in about three months and Sultan was tall, dark, gorgeous, and I hadn't missed, on our first meeting, the imprint his cock left in his Levi's.

I disrobed first, laid myself across the bed, and watched as he slipped off his white T-shirt and Gap jeans.

I had seen the tattoo on his neck. It said MOM. I thought that was sweet. By the time he was down to his boxers, Sultan the man was gone and what stood before me was an art mural with limbs.

There were lizards and Medusa-looking women tattooed all over his chest and down his arms. Written across his back in red, green, and gold was NIGGA 4 LIFE.

Artists' renditions of AK-47s graced both of his thighs.

"What the fuck!" I shouted as I popped straight up.

"What?" He gave me an amused look and flexed his biceps.

"What are those?" I shrieked, pointing a shaky finger at him.

"Tats."

" 'Tats'?"

"Tattoos, baby. Why you trippin'?"

"But so many?"

"Yeah, well, some of the other vics got more than this."

" 'Vics'?"

"Convicts."

"I—I don't understand."

"What don't you understand?"

"You were in jail?"

"I told you that, baby," he said, walking toward me, his dick already hard.

"No, you didn't."

"Yes, I did. I told you I did some time upstate."

"I thought you meant Binghamton, where the flagship store

of your company is located." I shrank back from his touch. I couldn't fuck a convict.

"Whatever," he said, and with that dismissed the whole thing. "Now take them goddamn thongs off, girl. I want to eat that ass." He snickered wickedly.

Eat my ass? What kind of sick shit was this?

"What?" I whispered, my heart racing.

"Rimming, girl, you know. Now get them off," he said, and then wagged the longest tongue I'd ever seen at me.

I was afraid to say no. I mean, maybe he'd done time for rape. No one likes a cock teaser, especially a hardened criminal with an erection.

I closed my eyes and felt his hands on my hips; his thumbs hooked into the waistband of my black net thong and slid it down and off.

"Turn over, babe," he whispered, his voice guttural now.

Turn over? Oh my God—he was going to do me prison-style!

Once on my stomach, I was stiff as a board—my fingers gripped my pillow and I squeezed my eyes tightly shut, waiting for the moment his big black cock would rip into me, but what I felt instead was his tongue on the nape of my neck. After a moment he dragged it down the length of my spine and then stopped at my lower back, where he began to nibble my skin.

I still wasn't able to relax.

"Damn, girl," he muttered breathlessly, "you got some kind of ass." Then I felt his lips on my left buttock and then my right. He spent more than fifteen minutes kissing and biting my plump behind. I would be a liar if I told you I hadn't started to enjoy it.

I was just beginning to relax when suddenly he smacked my ass.

My head popped up off the pillow. "What the——?" I cried, turning to look back at him.

"Ah yeah, *shiiiit*," he yelped, and slapped my ass again.

"Hey, that hurts," I protested, trying to flip myself over.

He held me firm. "I'm sorry, babe, forgive me," he cooed, and began kissing my behind again.

That was more like it.

I was starting to think that the kissing and nibbling was the extent of his lovemaking when he slid his hand down into the crack of my ass.

My body tensed.

His middle finger played around my "exit" hole, never penetrating, just teasing the rim. To my embarrassment I was as wet as a washrag back there. I didn't even know I could get wet there.

After a while he parted my cheeks and began to blow. I tell you something, I could have come right then and there!

And then, without any warning, his tongue slipped into me—into my hole!

In and out, in and out, in and out . . .

I was squirming like a newborn, squealing like a pig, bracing myself for the orgasm that was rushing from the pit of my gut.

When it hit, my body went stiff and then spastic. I gripped the pillow, lifted my head and bellowed, "Holy fucking shit!" and then collapsed into a stuttering, trembling mess.

Sultan breathed, moved his palms across my ass like it was a crystal ball, and announced proudly, "You have just been rimmed."

Turns out Sultan hadn't served time for rape, murder, or drugs. He'd written some bad checks when his mother was sick. But I ended it anyway. Sultan just didn't seem, well, he just didn't seem safe.

Next up was Henderson. I'd seen him on the subway in the morning. He always offered me a kind smile and a warm greeting. He looked like an accountant or a bookworm, with his neat haircut, dark suit, and horn-rimmed glases. Turns out he was both.

We went out on six dates before he even kissed me on the cheek.

He wasn't boring. Well, he was a little boring.

But it seemed as if we wanted the same things. Marriage, children, and a home with a white picket fence.

On our twelfth date, while we were having dinner at Red Bamboo, he presented me with a certificate of "authenticity"—well, what it really was was a clean bill of health. He'd taken an HIV test a few days earlier.

"Oh," I said, fingering the thin paper, more than a little stunned.

"Crystal Atkins," Henderson began in a quivering voice as he dropped down on one knee.

My breath caught in my throat and I thought: Oh God, he's going to propose!

"Would you allow me to make love to you?"

I breathed a sigh of relief and then laughed. "Yes, yes, Henderson, I will."

"Good, good," he said, rising to his feet and straightening the sharp seam in his slacks, and then, almost as an afterthought, he said, "Have you had an HIV test?"

Once again I was caught off guard. "Y-yes," I murmured. And I had, two years earlier.

"Recently?"

"Um, no," I said, feeling embarrassed.

"Well, I think you should, just to be safe."

And I did.

We made love at his place, on his double bed with the fake brass headboard.

He fucked like a rabbit. Rapidly.

He'd bang into me about thirty times, stop, take a breath, and then bang into me thirty more times. It went on like that for at least 150 thrusts before he let off a long whistle, shivered, collapsed, and muttered, "Damn."

Which would be the closest he'd ever come to swearing.

Did I mention that his dick was about as long and as thick as my index finger?

Afterward, I'd lie there staring up at the ceiling, wondering if I could spend the rest of my life with a rabbit fucker. It would be hard at first, but I'd keep my dildos—that would help. Maybe next time, I thought, we would make love at my house and I'd introduce him to my twin dildos, Jack and Johnny. Maybe next time I'd show him how making love is supposed to be done.

I snickered.

"What's that, Crystal?" Henderson mumbled sleepily.

"Nothing, baby. Just gas."

Three months in, I knew I couldn't take it anymore. The rabbit fucking, the conservative suit, the fake brass headboard—all of it.

I was going to break it off.

We were at Nobu, beautiful people buzzing all around us. Denzel Washington had been on his way out just as we walked in. I swear to God, I almost turned around and followed that man to his waiting sedan, but Henderson had a death grip on my hand.

I was picking at my sushi while Henderson methodically cut off pieces of his miso salmon and arranged it in an orderly fashion on his plate before he began to eat.

He only ate from left to right, and his meal was ruined if the food on his plate touched.

I watched him, hating him with every forkful of food he put in his mouth and resisting the urge to stab him in the eye with my chopsticks.

"So, Crystal, I was thinking."

He was always thinking.

"That maybe we should get married."

My eyes stretched wide. Had he lost his goddamn mind?

"I know, I know, it's sudden," he said, putting down his fork and picking up his napkin. He looked very pleased with himself, very smug. "But I've put a great deal of thought into this. I've done the numbers, and you and me, we add up."

You fuck like a rabbit! I wanted to scream.

"So what do you say?" Beaming, he reached into the breast pocket of his jacket and pulled out a small black velvet box.

I didn't want to see it, because if it was large and sparkly I might be dazzled enough to say yes.

Smiling, he slid it across the table. "I do hope you'll say yes."

Against my will, my shallow-minded right hand reached over and snatched up the box. My other hand, just as superficial, joined in, and before I knew it, the lid was up and I was looking at the

smallest

fucking

diamond chip I'd ever seen.

"No, Henderson. No, I don't think so," I happily responded as I pushed the box back across the table.

Five minutes later when the waiter brought the dessert menus, Henderson's mouth was still hanging open in shock. I skipped on the dessert and ordered myself a glass of champagne. Henderson and I were through. I needed to celebrate.

Geneva

· · · · · · · · · · · · · ·

Okay, so let me just get this out in the open, right from Jump Street: I weigh 230 pounds.

For the past year I've been quite comfortable with my bodacious body. Prior to that I'd been on every diet program known to man. But a little over a year ago I snagged one of the finest men I'd ever seen. I mean Idris Elba fine, and to top it off, he's a young thang.

Now lower your eyebrows and swallow that comment you want to sling at me about cradle robbing and any other negative euphemism you've got caught in the back of your throat, because I've heard it all and don't need to hear any more.

Oh, sorry—what, you were going to ask if the sex was good because you've got your eye on a young thang yourself?

Well, I'd be lying if I said it wasn't. It's the best sex I've ever had, and I've had a lot of sex. Believe me, Mother has had some sex!

But I digress.

So while this brother—his name is Deeka, by the way—was working hard to get next to me, I was pushing him away.

Why?

Because I couldn't believe that someone that looked like him was interested in me. Not that I think I'm unattractive, but he's gorgeous—Hollywood good-looking—a real specimen, if you know what I mean.

So anyway, there I was, blocking like I'd never blocked before, fending him off like the plague, but do you think that deterred him?

Not at all. He just kept coming back, doing everything and anything to get me to say, "Yeah, I'll go out with you."

Not that I didn't want him next to me, you understand. Shoot, since we're being all open and shit, laying it out on the table, as they say—I wanted nothing more than to have that man next to me. In fact, my fantasy was to have him up on top of me and inside of me—if you get my drift.

But what I didn't want was for him to see my dimpled thighs, the folds of blubber around my waist, and the unruly gray hairs that were springing up around my pleasure place, rapidly wiping out the shiny black ones of my youth.

I complained about it to my friend Noah and he just said, "Your fat ain't bothering no one but you, Geneva. Get over it and give the boy a chance."

Well, he had a point. I was the one obsessing about it, not Deeka. In fact, the only time it ever came up in conversation was when I brought it up, and then Deeka's stock response was "Baby, I love you just the way you are."

Yeah, we're in love.

So I gave Deeka the green light and am so glad I did. My life has changed in ways that I never imagined. For one, I'm happy most all of the time. I mean, there are those days when an ignorant customer may say or do something to upset me (I work at a diner, and ignorant customers are what keeps it in business), but other than that, I'm a ball of sunshine.

Recently, though, I've suffered a little setback.

My six-year-old daughter, Chartreuse, Charlie for short, participated in her school's talent show, and being the proud mama that I am, I went and took a seat right up in the front row.

My little girl was going to recite a poem. One she'd made up all on her own.

I politely applauded through the ten acts that came before her and then my Charlie strolled onto the stage, her little Vaseline-slathered face gleaming beneath the stage lights. I got all choked up, jumped up out of my seat, and yelled, "That's my baby! That's my baby girl!" even before the principal introduced her.

Principal Keane, a bald-headed white man with one blue eye and one green eye, cleared his throat loudly over the intercom and threw a stony warning at me with his eyes. I stopped clapping, apologized softly under my breath, and sat down.

"Miss Chartreuse Holliday will be reciting a poem titled 'Jelly,'" Principal Keane said.

I beamed, held my breath, and waited.

Charlie moved to the microphone, looked proudly at me, and bellowed:

My mother's belly
shakes like jelly!
My mother's belly

shakes like jelly!
Jelly, jelly, jelly!

I was horrified. I wanted to curl up and die right where I sat.

For a moment the auditorium was so quiet you could hear a pin drop. And I could feel more than see the dozens of eyes on me. Then the snickering began, followed by a loud guffaw, and then somewhere off in the distance I heard Principal Keane say, "Let's give Miss Holliday a round of applause for her original poem."

The clapping started in the back of the room. It was a slow, unsure clap that took about forty seconds to catch on until it became a thunderous applause that rolled like a wave through the audience.

Me, I was ten different shades of red. I wanted to get up and run from the building. I wanted to cry, but most of all I wanted to strangle that little crumb-snatcher formerly known as my daughter!

She'd shared our secret dance with the world.

The jelly dance was something I'd begun doing for her when she was just a toddler. She'd try her best to imitate me, and as she got older, she actually became really good at it.

It was something we both did in our underwear, up on our toes, arms flapping like wings, necks jerking like chickens, and stomachs wiggling and jiggling like jelly.

"Did you like it, Mommy?"

I was standing in a dark corner of the auditorium, trying my best to hide my face behind the open program I held in my hand. I looked down at my baby girl and had a horrific vision of slapping her so hard that her black face flew off and splattered against the wall behind her.

I bit down hard on my bottom lip, dug my hands into the pockets of my jeans, and said, "Yes, baby, I loved it."

So that brings me to what I really want to tell you. I haven't been able to get that little poem of Charlie's out of my head. Every time I undress, walk past a mirror, or catch a full-length view of myself in the pane-glass fronts of department stores, and even when I lie down with my man, all I can hear is "My mother's belly shakes like jelly. Jelly! Jelly! Jelly!"

I can't take it anymore.

I need to lose weight, and in order to accomplish that, I have to stop eating—or shall I say stop eating so much of what it is I eat. I also have to start exercising. But I barely have the energy to run behind Charlie and, thank God, most of the sex Deeka and I have takes place lying down.

The few times we did it standing up against the wall left me feeling like I'd run a mile instead of worked my way up to an orgasm.

So the way I see it, my situation is serious, and serious situations call for serious measures, and that's when I decided to call the number on the ad I'd ripped out of *Healthy Life* magazine, which I'd been flipping through at my gynecologist's office.

I'd had the glossy piece of paper tucked into my wallet for about a year. Every now and again I'd pull it out and read the declaration:

BIOTHIN NATURAL DIET PILLS
DO ALL THE WORK FOR YOU.

I was sold and ordered a two-month supply.

Which leads me to now. Here I am, pill in one hand, glass of water in the other, and hope in my heart that this will be my final battle in the war of the weight.

Wish me luck . . .

Gulp.

Noah

....

We didn't even make it to the bedroom.

We'd had a little tiff that morning before he left for work, leaving me angry all day long, and not everybody knows this about me, but being angry makes me horny, so when Zahn walked into the flat that evening I greeted him at the door buck naked.

"Oh, my," Zahn had said, and grinned when he looked down at my rock-hard erection.

I threw myself against him and began covering his face in kisses. Zahn lifted me up and I wrapped my legs around his back as I ripped at the dove gray Izod shirt he wore.

I'd worked myself into a sex-hungry frenzy. I was out of my mind with lust when I bit down into his lip. The taste of his blood in my mouth took me to a level I'd never been to before.

Zahn, unable to make it to the bedroom, turned right and

plopped me down onto the kitchen counter, where he carefully laid me back, kissed my navel, and then took my engorged penis into his mouth.

It didn't matter that we'd had sex on the kitchen counter and then down on the living room floor—I was still mad at him.

We lay naked on the Berber carpet, our backs facing each other. We were quiet, both knowing that we'd reached a crossroads in our relationship.

Some things had gone on over the past year that made me think that maybe I'd committed myself to the wrong man. Don't get me wrong, I love that skinny little white boy to death, but lately, I don't know, things have started to change.

It could be me, going through some midlife crisis; I will be forty this year.

I find myself searching for lines in my face, pushing myself harder at the gym, trying to stay away from carbohydrates and alcohol. I drink damn near a gallon of water a day and eat so many fruits and vegetables . . . Well, let's just say that constipation is a fading memory.

Zahn, he's not as health conscious as I am, but he should be; he's five years older than me. He spent his younger years dropping acid, smoking cigarettes, and drinking like a fish. He hasn't been kind to his body, and it's beginning to show.

When I first met him, he was smoking a pack a day. When we finally got together and I started to complain about it, he just didn't understand my aversion to it.

You see, in Europe, it's hard to find anyone who doesn't smoke. And those "Truth" commercials you see all over American television about what tobacco does to your body—well, those are nonexistent here.

Smoking is an acceptable way of life on this side of the Atlantic.

I finally got him to quit, but I suspect that he's picked it up again.

I smell it as soon as he walks through the door. He claims it's from the patrons in the pub he frequents before coming home from work. I never taste it on his tongue, but smoker's mints can be a powerful cloak.

One time when I was complaining and accusing him of picking up the nasty habit again, he turned on me and barked, "Maybe you've driven me to it."

I was stunned. Zahn hardly ever yelled at me.

While I stood there clutching my chest in shock, he stormed out of the flat and didn't return home until two the next morning.

Of course he reeked of scotch and Marlboros.

Okay, maybe I have driven him to smoking again. Maybe I am the cause of the tension between us.

You see, I went back on my word, but in my defense it was something I'd committed to in the throes of passion many years earlier. Okay, just three years earlier.

A child.

Zahn wanted a child, and when we decided that we would spend the rest of our lives together, I agreed that we would, in the future, adopt a little girl or boy. Or if that didn't work out, sign up for one of those turkey baster procedures where my sperm would be injected into some well-compensated willing female.

I agreed, because I love my man and the thought of being a complete family made him happy and I loved seeing my man happy.

But to tell the truth, I don't really like kids. I've got to be honest here. I love them from a distance, but I can't stand to be around them for more than an hour at a time. Babies are okay, but once they hit age two, don't bring them back around me until they turn eighteen and we can have a conversation.

Children are messy, loud, and needy. I have a beautiful flat here with very expensive furnishings and priceless pieces of art. For God's sake, what are we supposed to do, trade in our two-seater Mercedes for a minivan?

I am not the one. I like my life; a child would just ruin it.

When I voiced my opinion about the whole thing Zahn was quiet . . . For three days he was quiet while I walked around on eggshells, not knowing exactly what he was putting together in his mind.

When he finally did decide to speak—what do you think he spoke about?

Children!

"Noah, when we got together you agreed to this. Why are you going back on your word?"

"Did I really agree, Zahn? I just remember saying that it was a possibility."

"You agreed, Noah."

"Were we having sex at the time?" I teased. "You know I agree to anything when you have your dick up my—"

"Stop it, Noah!"

He stormed out of the house and was gone for most of the evening. When he returned he announced that he would be spending the summer in New Delhi.

"India?"

"Yes."

"But why?"

"They need me to oversee the opening of the new furniture factory."

"The whole summer?"

"Yes—it will be good for us, the separation. I think we both need time to think."

"You don't want me to come with you?"

"I think it will be best if you went back to New York. I'm sure your friends and family would love to see you, especially since you missed spending Christmas with them last year."

Zahn said all that while looking me straight in the eye. His stare was stone cold, his jaw tight. I was sure that this was the beginning of the end of us.

The thought of losing him made me feel sick to my stomach, but I wasn't about to budge on this. Not now, not ever.

"Oh, okay," I murmured, and walked away with my tail between my legs.

I needed to get away from this gloomy city any goddamn way. The rain, the chill, and the fucking cigarette smoke everywhere you turned. Come to think of it, I really didn't like London very much. New York would be a welcome change . . . maybe even a permanent one.

Chevy

∙∙∙∙∙∙∙∙∙∙∙

I lost my apartment a few years ago because a pair of Manolo Blahniks was more important to me than paying my rent. My childhood friend Noah allowed me to move into his three-story brownstone. Well, he didn't really allow me in—he kind of left me to house-sit and when he returned all my shit was there.

Noah is living in England now, and he only comes through once or twice a year and that's never for more than two or three weeks at a time. He tries to act as if he hates having me in his house (okay, sometimes I forget to pay him rent), but I know deep down inside he's glad to have me here because a vacant house ain't nothing but a big old yellow and green WELCOME sign for burglars.

I've got it pretty good. Anyone else would have a load of

money saved, but not me—to date I've maxed out both my Visa and MasterCard.

They were legitimate purchases. I have a high-profile position and need to dress the part. And anyway, designers should be paying me some type of commission for wearing their shit. I'm so fine, I make their clothes look good—not the other way around.

Now, American Express is a whole other story—I can't begin to tell you what's going on with that card. The best I can figure is either I blacked out somewhere last month and went on a spending spree or that little green and white card slipped from my wallet and went out on the town without me.

Six thousand dollars later, Mr. Hubert in collections is calling my job and cell day and night, leaving all kinds of threatening messages.

I told myself when I got my current job as a personal assistant to the high-profile radio personality Anja that I'd clear up my debt and open a savings account. I told myself that I would begin to act like an adult. And for a month or two, I did.

But keeping up with the Joneses ain't always an easy task. And keeping up with my boss, Anja, is even more difficult.

But first let me hip you on something that few people know: Anja is really a man, and I've been doing him on and off for a year now.

Oh, please, don't look so surprised—that woman sitting next to you on the train may be a man or vice versa.

In this world, people do what they need to do to get by or get over or just get famous. At the beginning of his career Andre started dressing in drag just for kicks—personally I really think he enjoys wearing women's underwear, but don't let that freaky shit fool you: he is all man when you get down to the nitty-gritty of it.

Why do I sleep with him, you ask?

What a stupid question. Women have been screwing their way to the top for centuries. Need I remind you of the power of pussy?

Pussy has felled empires, and I'm counting on mine to bring Andre to his knees. He's a fool because he believes that the seventy-five thousand dollars a year I'm getting, along with our hot sexual romps, is enough to keep me satisfied and in my place.

I want his job, his money, and his fame, and I have no doubt that I will get it. It's going to take some time and planning, but I'm willing to make sacrifices and may even blow the whistle on his cross-dressing ass to get it.

The only obstacle in my way is Dante. Dante is the flame that hired me. We were cool in the beginning, but then he realized that Anja was favoring me over him and he lost his ever-loving mind.

We had a fight in a club last year and I'm sure we both thought we would be fired, but what Anja did was reassign Dante as my assistant.

A fate worse than death for him. I'm sure if he didn't have eight designer dogs and two Egyptian felines to feed and house, he would have quit his job right then and there rather than work under me.

I know I could be a vindictive bitch at times, but I gotta tell you, I was afraid for my life.

Every time I looked at Dante, his eyes were throwing daggers at me even though he was smiling.

It got so bad that each morning when I arrived at my office, I checked under my desk and my chair for homemade bombs.

Eventually, though, Anja reassigned him yet again and contact between Dante and me tapered down to nothing.

I see him in meetings every now and again and I see the way he looks at Anja—his eyes are filled with nothing but loathing for her and I fear that he might "out" her before I get the chance to.

April

Crystal

· · · · · · · · · · · · · ·

It was eight-thirty in the morning and I'd just stepped out of the shower. I should have been at work already, but these days I was as slow as a turtle. I just didn't have any energy at all. I was just two months from my fortieth birthday, but my body felt like it was about to turn seventy.

Sighing, I reached for the alcohol-soaked cotton ball and dabbed at the two new pimples on my chin. The acne from my teen years had returned with a vengeance—not only that, but my once glowing skin had taken on a dull, faded look and I was developing dark circles beneath my eyes.

I hadn't been sleeping well, even though most days I worked like a dog and came home dead on my feet. I almost always went directly to bed but would eventually wake up with a start in less than three hours and spend the rest of the night tossing and turning or watching seventies sitcom reruns on Nick at Nite. By the time five-thirty a.m. came around I was just slipping back into la-la land.

Back in the day I would hop out of bed, do my crunches and a few stretches, and then take a forty-five-minute run through the park. Now all I had energy enough for was to hit the snooze button and try to catch forty or so more winks.

My position as a director at the Ain't I A Woman Foundation was on shaky ground. I was arriving to work late almost every day, and it was just April and I'd already taken two of my five weeks' vacation, four sick days, and two personal days.

I won't even get into the half days, the extended lunch hours, and the hours I've spent locked in my office, behind my desk, tilted back in my chair and staring out the window.

If daydreaming counted for billable hours, I'd be rich.

My boss, Mr. Fisher, a small, gray-haired, stout white man in his early sixties, had called me into his office just yesterday. We'd known other for nearly fifteen years. I was his secretary at the Rockefeller Foundation, and when he got the position at Ain't I A Woman, he took me with him but explained to me that he did not expect me to manage his day planner, answer his phone, and make his coffee for the rest of my life. He expected me to spread my wings, take the bull by the horns, and make a career for myself.

And I'd done just that, taking on a new position every eighteen months until finally I was promoted to director of housing.

Mr. Fisher was senior director over all areas of the foundation, so after fifteen years he was still my boss.

"Lovely to see you, Crystal." Adolph Fisher came from around his desk and greeted me with a tight hug and warm kiss to my cheek. The greeting was not proper office decorum, but Mr. Fisher, or Adolph as I called him when we were alone, had been more than just a boss and a mentor; he had been on many levels a father figure to me.

I hugged him back.

"Sit down, sit down," Adolph said, indicating the black leather club chair to his left. Adolph himself did not take his swivel seat behind the massive glass office desk; instead, he sat in the matching leather club beside me, turned his big blue eyes on me, reached over, took my hand in his, and said, "I don't know what's going on with you, but you know I love you like you were my flesh and blood, and because I do . . ."

Adolph stopped there for a moment and gave me a penetrating look before he went on.

"I need to be frank with you and advise you that your job is in jeopardy, and if you don't straighten up, I'm going to have to let you go."

I just broke down, sobbing like a baby for damn near fifteen minutes. Mr. Fisher, Adolph, gave me a box of Kleenex and patiently waited for my waterworks to drizzle down to heaves and nose blowing.

He had a wife and five daughters; emotional outbursts were familiar territory for him.

"I-I'm sorry, Adolph. I—" I blubbered.

"No need to be sorry, Crystal."

"I just don't know what's gotten into me. I—I just don't know," I cried through a fresh stream of tears.

And I didn't know. Things were happening to my body that I just did not understand. The gray hairs were a shock, but then the on-again-off-again menstrual cycle had really sent me for a loop. The excessive bloating I could handle, but these sudden emotional outbursts were really getting on my nerves.

Lately, it don't take much to get me weeping; a Hallmark

commerical or the arrival of an invitation to a wedding or, worse yet, a baby shower was usually all it took to send me over the edge.

"Could it be menopause?" Adolph said.

My reaction was one of shock and surprise. My head snapped back on my neck and my mouth dropped open. How dare he say something like that to me? We were familiar, yes, but shit, Adolph had crossed the line!

I wiped at my tears, cleared my throat, and smoothed my hands across the material of my skirt before saying in a tight tone, "Adolph."

He put his hands up, not in surrender but in defense of his statement.

"Crystal, you know Elaine, my first daughter, went through menopause at the age of thirty-two. It's rare, but not unheard of."

I bit down on my bottom lip. I had considered that but had quickly ushered that thought from my mind. I couldn't be menopausal; I hadn't had a child yet. God wouldn't do something like that to me. Or would he?

Adolph continued, "Lucky for Elaine, she'd had Billy and Rebecca in her twenties."

I could give a shit about Elaine and her two blue-eyed, blond-haired children! I could give a rat's ass! I didn't have a child, nor did I have a prospect for a man that could give me a child—all I had was this fucking job, an overpriced apartment, and a retirement account that had taken a $30,000 hit this month.

I didn't have a husband and a family like Elaine. As far as I was concerned, Elaine had everything and I had nothing.

"Yes, lucky for Elaine," I mumbled, and even managed a smile as I casually slipped my hand from his. Clearing my throat and wiping at the last vestiges of tears clinging to my cheeks, I straightened my back and tried to recapture the dignity I had entered that room with.

"It's just PMS, Adolph, and a small iron deficiency, that's all," I said abruptly as I rose to my feet.

Adolph didn't look convinced. We'd known each other too long. "If you say so, Crystal," he offered quietly as he too rose to his feet.

I extended my hand. "Thank you for taking the time to speak to me, and again, forgive me for the outburst."

Adolph looked at my hand as if he didn't know what to do with it, and then he looked at me. I saw the hurt swimming in his eyes. My formality had wedged a space between us. "My door is always open, Crystal," he said, and finally shook my hand.

That was yesterday. Now it was Friday morning, and I was late and still carrying the shame of the day before. I walked into my bedroom, picked up the cordless, dialed my office, and told my assistant that I would not be coming in today.

I placed the receiver back down on the base and stared at it for a moment. My mind questioned, calculated, whirled, and spun before finally coming to a halt.

A decision had been made. I picked the receiver up again and pressed speed dial number eight. After two short rings, the computer-generated voice said: *Thank you for calling American Airlines—if you are a frequent flyer member, press one now.*

Geneva

....

So are you sure you'll be coming in on that day?" I asked Noah as I stood in the kitchen, clutching my robe together with one hand while I moved my Newport to and from my mouth with the other.

"Yes, I'm all confirmed," Noah screeched from the other end of the line.

"Okay, I just want to make sure, because I want to cook you a welcome home dinner since you missed spending Christmas with us."

"Okay, Geneva—you said that like ten times. Damn."

"Oh, have I?"

"Yes, girl—you going senile on me or something?"

I had been a little absentminded lately.

"Anyway," I started, completely ignoring his comment, "I'll let the girls know and—"

"Don't tell Chevy. I want to surprise Ms. Drama, catch her off guard."

"Hmm—she owe you rent money?"

"You know it!"

"Noah, I don't know why—"

"Look, Geneva, I have got to run now. See you in a few weeks—ta-ta."

"Okay, bye, Noah," I said, and pressed the End button on the phone. After I stubbed my cigarette out in the ashtray I hurried into the bathroom. I needed to weigh myself to see just how much I'd lost.

I removed my robe, tossed it to the floor, and jumped eagerly onto the scale.

228.

I'd only lost two pounds in one month.

Jumping angrily off the scale, I flopped down onto the toilet lid, rocking the commode on its porcelain base.

It wasn't fair, not at all. I'd expected to shed at least ten pounds by now.

I shot an angry glance at the bottle of Biothin that sat on the sink counter.

Snatching up the bottle, I peered at the directions:

TAKE ONE PILL BEFORE EACH MEAL.

I'd been doing that. I threw the bottle across the room and it hit the wall and fell to the ground, sending little yellow pills scurrying across the floor.

Child protection safety cap my ass.

I put my robe back on and stormed out of the bathroom and over to the computer, which sat on a small square folding table near the living room window. I had DSL now, thanks to my boyfriend, Deeka. I pointed the blinking cursor to the tab that was marked Favorites.

Biothin was at the top of the list. I clicked on that and was taken directly to the Web site. I read and reread all the information, including the testimonials. I stared hard at the before-and-after pictures. Everyone looked fabulous, so why wasn't it working for me?

I began to sulk.

Okay, I hadn't totally given up Ben and Jerry's ice cream, and so I still enjoyed a Krispy Kreme donut every day with my coffee, and I loved me some hot biscuits and gravy, and Friday night was still pizza and Corona night, but still . . . two pounds?

I looked toward the bathroom, where the pills were still scattered across the floor.

Maybe I should take two before each meal?

I started toward the bathroom.

Two pills would really kick-start my system. I've always had a slow system, slow blood—at least that's what my mother always said.

No, no, I remember now—it was tired blood. Well, tired blood would be slow, wouldn't it? And medicine moved through your blood system, didn't it? And if I had tired, slow blood wouldn't it take a long time for the stuff in the pills to get to the fat?

I think it would, and who knows how much medicine was still in the pill by the time it got there. Maybe it wasn't enough to do what it was supposed to do. Maybe two pills would guarantee results. Two is always better than one, right?

I gathered the pills from the floor and dropped them lovingly back into the bottle. That's what I'll do, I thought as I went into the kitchen and pulled the two-liter bottle of Pepsi from the refrigerator. I'll take two pills from now on.

"What's that, Mommy?" Charlie's small voice came from behind me, startling me so that I almost spit up the mouthful of Pepsi.

I wiped my mouth with the back of my hand and hurriedly shoved the soda back into the fridge before turning around to face her.

"What's what, pumpkin?"

"Those," she said pointing her finger at the bottle of Biothin clutched in my hand.

"Oh," I breathed, giving the bottle a quick shake before placing it on top of the refrigerator, safely out of Charlie's reach. "Those are—are my, um, magic beans!" I squealed triumphantly.

Charlie made a face. "Magic beans?"

"Yes, yes," I said, taking her by the hand and leading her to the kitchen table.

"Like 'Jack and the Beanstalk'?"

"Exactly," I said as I pulled out the chair and helped her take a seat.

"Why are you eating them, Mommy?" Charlie's voice climbed—she was panicking. "If you eat them a tree will start to grow in your belly and—"

I place a calming hand on Charlie's shoulder. "No, sweetie, these are different. These magic beans will help Mommy to lose weight."

Chevy

· · · · · · · · · · · ·

I leaned back into the leather of my office chair and yawned.
I was exhausted. Friday couldn't have come fast enough, because I'd had a hell of a week.

Anja, my boss and lover, had worked me to the bone this
week—in and out of bed!

We'd hosted three parties at the celebrity hangout Bungalow
8. Each event had gone on to three a.m. in the morning, after
which Anja hopped in her limo and was whisked away to her Upper East Side condo.

Me, I would get in a yellow cab and get there about fifteen
minutes behind her, using my key to let myself in. Anja was always in the middle of removing what I'd come to call his Hal-
loween costume.

By the time we'd meet up in the marble shower, Anja was just a memory and Andre and I would create more steam than the fourteen water jets going full blast!

Now Friday was here and it was three o'clock. Upper management and executive assistants—that was me—could knock off early.

I pulled my purple Salvatore Ferragamo crocheted bag from the bottom drawer, hit the button on the computer monitor, and was up and out the door.

I found a space in the hallway crowded with other executives who were buzzing about all the sun they planned to soak up out in the Hamptons that weekend, and my BlackBerry started to vibrate. I dug into my bag and saw that there was a message from Anja.

Chevy please come to my office.

I sighed. I had been just seconds from a clean getaway.

"Enter," Anja's raspy voice ordered after I'd rapped lightly on her office door.

Stepping into the red and cream Asian-inspired office, I found Anja seated behind her desk and a voluptuous red-haired vixen seated before her.

"Chevanese Cambridge, meet LaTangie Fox, my new assistant."

Her words hit me like a ton of bricks. New assistant? Why the fuck did she need another assistant? She had five too many already.

I forced a smile and glided across the floor toward LaTangie, extending my hand. "Hello, so nice to meet you," I said as I took in her flawless cream-colored skin and petite nose. She smiled, dazzling me with her blindingly white teeth.

My eyes rolled over her. She was certainly very well put together dressed in a dark blue Antonio Melani suit. This LaTangie
chick had good taste; I had the same suit in coral.

"Same here," LaTangie responded.

I'd detected an accent. "Southern?" I inquired.

"Louisiana, to be exact. My daddy is French," she drawled.
"White," she added and smiled. "My mama is Creole."

Did I ask for all that?

"That's nice," I said, and moved my gaze to Anja, who was
smiling smugly at me.

"LaTangie just graduated from Columbia," Anja announced
like a proud mother.

I nodded and mumbled, "That's nice" again as I looked down
at my watch.

"Are we keeping you from something, Chevy?" Anja asked.

"Chevy? Oh, that is just an adorable nickname," LaTangie
piped.

I looked at her and had to suppress the urge to smack her
across her pretty face. "My nickname is Tan-gee."

I smirked, already sick of her Southern cadence.

"Anything else, Anja?" I said briskly. Anja had an amused
look on her face.

"Anja was just informing LaTangie of her duties," Anja said,
glancing down at her Lee Press On Nails. "She will be moving
into Dante's office, right across from you."

My mouth fell open.

"Where's Dante going?"

Anja gave me a bored look and drummed her plastic nails on
the glass desk. "He's no longer working at La Fleur Industries."

My heart seized up in my chest. Sure, Dante and I had had

our share of problems, and yes, he had been a thorn in my side at times, and of course him being gone made me next in line for Anja's position, but even with all that, something about this whole situation gave me a bad feeling in my gut.

I was more than sure that if Dante had found a position with another company there would have been at the very least some sort of farewell party, or balloon bouquet, something, anything. He'd been with Anja for ten years, for chrissakes!

Had Anja just disposed of Dante? Could I be next in line? I braced myself and asked, "Was he let go?"

Anja let out a small laugh, waved her hand at me, and said, "Anja would like you to show LaTangie to her office."

I nearly choked. "What?"

"Don't make Anja repeat herself," Anja practically barked at me.

I looked stupidly at LaTangie, who had popped up out of her chair like a jack-in-the-box.

"Oh, that's so nice of you, Chevy," she said, and beamed as she slipped her arm through the straps of her Furla pocketbook. "Now we can have some time to really get to know each other."

I didn't want to get to know her.

"Bye-bye, Anja, and thank you so much for the opportunity. I will do you and La Fleur Industries proud!" LaTangie said, and saluted Anja.

I might be wrong, but I saw a twinkle in Anja's eye. I'd seen that twinkle a number of times as I undressed.

LaTangie turned to me and said, "Ready, Freddie!"

Ugh, what a Southern-fried cornball.

· · ·

"This is beautiful," LaTangie squealed as we stood in the center of her new office. It was beautiful, with its plum-colored walls and emerald green accent furniture.

Like my office, this one also had an in-suite marble bathroom complete with bidet.

I was about to excuse myself when LaTangie turned toward me and said, "Damn, looks like I hit motherfucking pay dirt!"

My heard jerked with surprise.

LaTangie lifted her right hand into the air and said, "This office is the bomb, girl, give me some dap—we livin' large, yo!"

My mouth dropped open. LaTangie Fox was nothing more than a ghetto rat!

I took a hesitant step backward.

"You gonna leave me hanging like that? A'ight, sis, I'll remember that when I'm running this shit."

I just blinked. I couldn't believe the transformation that had taken place right before my eyes. There was no way in hell Anja would have hired a lowlife chickenhead like her.

LaTangie turned toward the row of floor-to-ceiling windows, spread her arms out at her sides, and yelled, "I'm on top of the world, Ma!"

Me, I got the hell out of there.

Crystal

· · · · · · · · · · · · · ·

I hadn't told Geneva that I would be flying out Saturday, which was tomorrow. I figured I owed it to her to give her the news face-to-face.

So here I sit at the Blue Water Grill, awaiting her arrival.

I'd purposely put off telling her because she always got so stressed out whenever any of us flew, especially now that her boyfriend and son were darting around the globe.

She was afraid that we'd all go down in flames, leaving her alone in the world. I figured if one of us could get her on a plane, she'd shake that fear.

I also delayed telling her because she was far from thrilled about my continued relationship with Neville. She liked him well enough but just thought it didn't make any sense to continue flying down to Antigua to be with him, since it was clear he wasn't interested in settling down, and sleeping with women was eighty percent of his livelihood.

Yeah, he's a gigolo.

He doesn't like that term, but no matter how you call it, it all means the same thing.

Neville likes to think of himself as a therapist, lover, and physical trainer all wrapped up in one. He claims he could take an emotional wreck of a woman, a woman with no self-esteem, and in less than a week send her home with so much confidence that one could see it spilling from her pores.

And he could. I'm walking proof of that.

He didn't come into my life because I was low on self-esteem—he came into my life because I'd been celibate, and celibacy—for me, anyway—turns into bitchiness, something my mother, Peyton, just could not deal with.

So, as outlandish as it may sound to you, my mother (with the assistance of Noah) arranged it so that Neville would visit with me and, well, to put it plain and simple, fuck me.

I have to admit that when I found out about what they'd done—all of them, including Neville—I was not a happy camper. But what was done was done, and the reality of it was that Neville was a real cool guy.

We laughed a lot together, and I had a genuine deep affection for him and the island of Antigua. I didn't know if it was Neville or the island that made me feel alive, safe, and calm. Maybe it was a combination of the two. Whatever it was, I was addicted and in need of a fix.

I looked at my watch; Geneva was already fifteen minutes late. I ordered a glass of wine and passed the time by watching the other patrons around me. To my left a young couple sat across the table from each other, holding hands and grinning foolishly into each other's eyes. To the right an older couple, salt-and-pepper hair, sat side by side, smiling and whispering to each other.

I could tell just from their body movements that they'd been together for years. They looked so in love, so happy.

I dragged my eyes away and forced back the feeling of self-pity that was welling up inside me.

I concentrated instead on Geneva and the situation at hand.

I'd have to choose my words carefully. She'd seemed overly sensitive lately. Maybe it was because Deeka and her son, Eric, had been on the road for nearly a month and I'd been too wrapped up in my own dismal life to spend any time with her.

Noah was in London, and she and Chevy never did the one-on-one thing. They loved each other, but their tolerance for each other was almost nonexistent.

And anyway, Geneva couldn't afford to go to any of Chevy's haunts, and Chevy didn't feel that Geneva was sophisticated enough to go to the corner store with her.

But I'd noticed that since Geneva had started dating Deeka, her sophistication altitude had climbed a few levels. She was now able to order wine by the label and her palate had expanded to include food other than fried chicken and smothered pork chops. She'd even started to read more, albeit those booty-slapping-gun-wielding-drug-pushing-baby-momma-drama-ghetto-life-glorification books, but reading is reading, I guess.

I was concerned about her weight, because in the month Deeka had been gone, she'd gained quite a few pounds, even though she claimed she was on some new diet regimen.

"Hey, girl!" Geneva rushed in like a storm. Her greeting boomed through the restaurant.

"Hey, mama," I said, and then my breath caught in my throat. "What the hell happened to your hair?"

"Girl, I just got up the other morning and whacked it off," she said brightly, throwing her hands up in the air before wrapping her fat arms around me. She reeked of Jean Naté.

When we broke the embrace I took a step back in order to take her all in.

For the past twenty years Geneva had worn her hair pulled back into a rinky-dink ponytail. Every now and again she'd get one of the girls in her building to throw some extensions in, but the ponytail had been her signature do since high school.

"You like?" she said, spinning in place.

I did.

The short Afro fit her melon-shaped face. "I do. It suits you."

We sat and Geneva began to talk about everything—I'd never heard so many run-on sentences in my life. It was as if she'd snorted cocaine or had too much Pepsi.

I looked on with amazement. Geneva's mouth was moving a mile a minute, and not only that—as she talked her hands flailed about as if she had no control over them, while her left leg bounced rapidly beneath the table.

I removed my cloth napkin from my lap and waved it frantically in her face.

"Geneva, time out," I said. "What's up with you?"

"What?"

"You're going a mile a minute. Shoot, I haven't said a word and I'm tired."

Geneva face unfolded. "Am I?" She giggled. "Oh, I guess I'm just excited to see you. It's been a while."

It had been a minute since we'd spent time together.

The waiter approached and Geneva ordered a Diet Pepsi.

"How's that going?" I asked.

"What?"

"The diet, silly."

"Oh, it's slow going—you know how it is. Anyway, what's going on with you?" she asked as she plucked a whole-grain roll from the bread basket.

"Well, I um, I'm going down to Antigua—"

"Again!" Geneva wailed and threw the roll down onto her plate. Her lip turned in and her eyes went dark.

You would have thought I told her I was sleeping with her man, the way she was glaring at me.

"Yes, again," I said, reaching for my wineglass. "Tomorrow," I added.

"Tomorrow!" she shrieked, and the elderly couple shot us an annoyed look.

"Keep your voice down, Geneva," I demanded through clenched teeth. "Stop making a scene."

Geneva gave me a long, hard look and then her face went slack and the tears started to roll. "I-I'm sorry, Crystal, I'm sorry," she blubbered.

Noah

· · · · · · · · · · ·

aybe she's premenopausal or something?" I suggested to Crystal. "I hear that makes women crazy."

"I dunno, Noah—I mean, she was crying like someone had died."

"Look, girl, don't let Miss Geneva and her mood swings spoil your little getaway. You go on to Antigua and have yourself a fucking good time—oh, I don't have to tell you that. That's your whole purpose of going, to have a fuck—"

"Okay, Noah." Crystal giggled. "I get it already."

"Call me when you get back, okay?"

"Will do."

Crystal and I said our goodbyes and I hung up the phone and turned to look at Zahn, who was brooding in the corner of the living room. He was sitting in the chair, legs crossed, staring out the window. We hadn't said more than two words to each other all day. Things between us were getting worse.

"Hey, babe," I called over to him, "how about we go out for dinner tonight? Maybe that new place on North End Road."

Zahn grunted but didn't look at me.

I started toward him. I just wanted us to get back to who we used to be before all this baby talk started pulling us apart.

"It's called 1492. You know, babe—Gerta and Shawn have done nothing but rave about the paella."

Gerta and Shawn were the new couple living above us. It seemed all the two of them did was screw and eat, eat and screw. We'd been begging them for months now to lay down carpet so we didn't have to hear the thumping and bumping of their excessive lovemaking.

I eased myself down onto Zahn's lap, took hold of his chin, and turned his face toward me. Zahn's eyes met mine for a brief moment before dropping away. They were empty. It seemed as though all the love he had for me had drained out of him. His lap was stiff beneath my legs, and he couldn't even find it in him to wrap his arms around me.

"Zahn?"

Was this really happening to us?

Zahn gently pushed me from his lap, rose from his chair, and walked to the bedroom, where he quietly shut the door behind him.

I stood there, my mouth open, hands on my hips, in shock.

This *was* really happening to us.

Chevy

. . . .

What the hell was Anja up to?

She was up to no good, that's what! I could feel it in my bones.

Anja never introduced a new employee to me, not ever. And what of Dante—where had he been banished off to? I thought as I stormed down the street and toward Melu-Melu.

Melu-Melu was the gym owned by La Fleur Industries, our parent company. It was an exclusive gym, where regular members paid one thousand dollars a month and were entitled to two free full-body massages every twenty days, as well as unlimited access to the organic juice and fruit bar, as well as three sessions a month with a personal trainer.

Membership for La Fleur employees was two thousand dollars a year. La Fleur employees were on the honor system and were required to make installment payments at their discretion as long as they were paid in full by the end of the calendar year.

Melu-Melu was frequented by the behind-the-scenes crowd. People you wouldn't know were "important" from looking at them because they were the power brokers behind the celebrities, the ones that wanted to have the *ka-ching*—without the *ka-problems* and publicity that come along with it.

These people were very rarely photographed and the *Post*'s Page Six didn't even know who they were.

I pushed open the rose-colored glass doors and walked across the marble reception area and up to the black granite counter. Pulling my ID from my wallet, I waved it in front of the scanner.

What normally followed was a chime of sorts, and then the metal arms would swing open, allowing me to pass through to the work area. But today a croaking sound resonated and I looked up to see the right eyebrow of the Japanese receptionist, sitting high on his forehead.

His eyes went to the flat-screen monitor in front of him.

"Try again, please."

I did and got the same croaking sound. "Let me see your card, Ms. Cambridge," he said, smiling.

I handed him the translucent card and sucked my teeth in disgust. I wanted him to know that I was annoyed.

"Please step to the side, Ms. Cambridge," he said, indicating the line that had formed behind me.

"What is it, bent or something?" I asked, standing on my tippy toes, trying to see what had come up on the computer screen. The receptionist was fumbling in an open drawer.

"No, not bent," he said, retrieving a pair of scissors. "Declined." He began snipping my card to shreds.

"What the fuck are you doing!" I shrieked as I tried to lunge for my card. The receptionist used the scissors to point at the sign on the west wall that stated NO PROFANITY, PLEASE.

"Your account is seriously delinquent," the receptionist began. "When you catch up, we will issue you a new card. Until then, I'm sorry," he said, shrugging his shoulders.

"You're not serious. I work for La Fleur Industries—they own this place!" I screamed. The receptionist just stared. "I am the personal—" I shouted, raising my index finger for emphasis, "personal assistant to Anja!"

"That's nice," he mumbled.

"Is this some type of joke?"

I just couldn't believe that this was happening to me. All the work I'd done for that fucking company. All the hours I'd clocked under that slave driver Anja.

"No, it's not, Ms. Cambridge. Now please lower your voice and leave the premises before I have to call security."

My mouth snapped shut. This must be a dream. I pinched myself. "Ow." I guess it wasn't. I folded my arms across my chest. "Call the security, 'cause I ain't going no-fucking-where."

Crystal

·········

the pilot announced that the flight attendants should prepare for landing. I closed my book and pressed the button along the sidearm of my seat, sending the back of my chair erect.

Outside my window was the blue Caribbean ocean, and wedged in the middle of all that aquamarine glory was Antigua. My heart leapt in my chest as the excitement I had suppressed for most of the four-hour trip began to bubble up inside of me. In just fifteen minutes we would touch down.

As soon as the Fasten Seat Belt sign went black, passengers jumped from their seats and began popping open the overhead luggage compartments. It would be another five minutes or so before the hatch would open.

I remained seated, sliding my hands across the shiny cover of my paperback. I would not cram my body into the aisle like my fellow passengers. I would not. I would not. I told myself this even as I felt my behind lifting from the seat and then wrenched myself between a Korean couple who had five different types of cameras hanging from straps about their necks.

As I reached for the carry-on I'd stored overhead, my elbow barely missed blinding the elderly gentleman who'd made his way beside me.

I wasn't fooling anyone but myself. I was just like the rest of them. I wanted out of the plane and into Antigua's glorious sunshine. But like all good things, a wait would be involved, first this one, then the mile-long lines at immigration, then luggage, and finally, customs.

I shifted my weight from foot to foot. The captain had turned off the air-conditioning. Perspiration was trickling down my underarms, gathering around my temples, springing from my scalp. A baby cried behind me in row thirty-seven, someone yawned loudly, and a young green-eyed boy meekly asked, "Mommy, what are we waiting for?"

Finally the hatch opened and the people closest to the door rushed forward but were halted by the petite hand of the first-class flight attendant. Her passengers would file off first. They had paid triple what we coach passengers had paid. They were royalty and we were but the lowly subjects.

Twenty of them—most clutching straw hats and over fifty-five.

The women, their chicken necks draped in gold and fingers lavished with diamonds, expensive coral-colored lipstick smeared across their lips, chattered happily as they walked ahead of their husbands.

The men, dressed in khakis and flowing linen shirts or T-shirts that declared their love for some other vacation destination, followed obediently behind.

They owned homes in Antigua, beachfront property with perfect views, 365 beaches—a beach for every day of the year.

Finally it was time for the coach passengers to disembark.

My stomach churned. I was starving, I was excited, I was queasy with joy!

When I stepped out onto the metal staircase, the heat wrapped itself around me. The air was heavy with the sweet scents of hibiscus, coconut, and the Caribbean Sea.

Before my feet touched the black tarmac, the grimy stress of New York had already slipped away. I could stay here forever, I thought, feeling my insides glow. I could quit my job and live happily ever after. Leave everyone and everything behind, throw caution to the wind—say fuck you and dump my old life for this new one!

"Fuck you!" I said aloud.

A woman in front of me turned around and said, "Pardon?"

"Not you." I laughed and placed a comforting hand on her shoulder. "New York."

"Indeed," she said, and winked at me.

Half an hour at immigration. A dark fellow with graying temples and bright teeth flipped through my passport and looked up at me. "Sixth time, huh?"

"Yes."

"What keeps you coming back?" His question was tinged with innuendo. He knew what kept me coming back. The island, the simple lifestyle, had seduced me. Okay, yes, and the man.

"The weather." I smiled.

He shot me a sly smile and stamped my passport. "I'll be at

the Boat House Bar at the harbor, if you ever get lonely," he whispered as he handed my passport back to me.

"I'll keep that in mind."

And I would.

I was someone different here in Antigua. I was a short skirt–wearing, bustier-toting vamp. At least that's how I saw myself. When I was on the island I felt sexy in a way that being in New York had never allowed me to feel.

I was feeling it now and tossed my hair casually over my shoulder as I offered a soft smile to a man who stood watching me from the other side of the carousel. His wife was chatting endlessly on her cell phone.

Possibilities all around me, and who would know if I met with the immigration officer? Who would know if I fucked the married man with the attention deficit wife? No one but me! This was my reality show and I was the only one who had access to the channel.

I plucked my suitcase from the carousel and set it down beside my feet. I had one more bag left and looked behind me to see how long the customs line was.

The tourists never queued up on the line "Items to Declare" even though they were coming in with American food products and electronics.

They sailed, smiling, through the "Nothing to Declare" line while casting quick glances at the residents of the islands, whose luggage was being opened and dumped on the large tables so customs officials could go through their belongings like mad dogs.

The second bag rolled around and I made my way to the "Nothing to Declare" line.

The stone-faced customs inspector peered at my declaration form and glanced at the green passport I clutched in my hand before checking me out from head to foot and then nodding that it was okay for me to pass.

I was outside. Back out beneath that glorious sky. Oh God, it felt good! It felt better than good: it felt perfect.

"Hey, gal." Neville's voice came from the left of me. I turned, then rushed and threw myself into him.

"I missed you too, baby." He laughed.

Geneva

• • • • • • • • • • • • • •

I'd been sitting, crying and smoking, since five a.m.

At around three o'clock I'd suddenly jumped straight out of my sleep. "What have I done?" I yelped in the darkness as I reached for the lamp switch. Directly across from my bed were my dresser and mirror. My reflection looked back at me. My short Afro was matted to one side. I looked horrible!

"My hair!" I wailed. Why had I done this to myself—why, why! What had possessed me to cut my hair off?

I leapt from the bed, pacing the floor and pulling at the short kinky strands. I looked at my reflection again; I looked like a man, or a straight-up dyke!

Now I looked even bigger, rounder, fatter! Deeka was going to flip, totally freak out, when he saw me. It was over. I knew he would take one look at me and end it.

"Waaaaaaaaaaaaaaaaaaaaa!"

I could fix it, right? I could get Shenika from the third floor to put some extensions in. Yeah, yeah. Long braids, right down my back, to my ankles, down to the friggin' floor!

That's what I would do. As soon as the sun came up I would call her and make an appointment.

I laughed out loud at my foolishness and then snickered at my ingenuity as I climbed back into bed and turned off the lamp. An hour later my eyes were still open and my heart was racing. Another hour passed and sleep was nowhere in sight.

I climbed out of bed again and lumbered into the kitchen and then to the fridge. Two glasses of Diet Pepsi later, I was sad again.

I looked at the clock; Crystal would be on her way to the airport now. I reached for the yellow wall phone. I would call and wish her a good trip, a safe trip. I pressed the first three numbers of her cell phone and then my mind clicked.

Why should I wish her anything?

She knew that Deeka and Eric wouldn't be home for another three weeks. Couldn't she have waited until they came back? She was selfish. Selfish and stupid! Who in their right mind would keep flying down to see a man who was clearly unavailable? He was using her, that's what he was doing, and Crystal was too stupid to see it.

Well, she deserves whatever she gets, which will probably be a disease!

I slammed the phone down again.

Later for her! She wasn't nothing but a flat leaver anyway.

After pacing the apartment for twenty minutes I decided to do some cleaning. There was dust everywhere, and I couldn't remember the last time I'd scrubbed the bathroom tile.

I turned on the radio and the apartment filled with music. The

DJ was playing old-school jams, and I was bopping my head to McFadden and Whitehead's ever-popular tune "Ain't No Stoppin' Us Now" when the phone rang.

I reached for the phone with one hand and turned down the volume on the radio with other.

"Hello?"

"Hey, baby, how you doing?" Deeka's voice came to me as if from the far end of a long hallway instead of where he actually was, which was thousands of miles away in Saudi Arabia.

"Deeka?"

I was so happy to hear from him I immediately became choked up.

"Are you all right, baby? You sound like you've been crying. What's wrong?"

"I'm okay," I said, wiping at my eyes and clearing my throat.

Of course everything wasn't okay with me. Men are so stupid. How could everything be okay?

Was he here?

Was my son here?

No, they weren't, and neither was my best friend either. Everybody was gone. I was all alone.

"Yeah, I'm fine. Is Eric there with you?"

"Nah, baby, he's out on the town."

My own son couldn't find the time to call me, his mother. I was the one who'd laid up on a hospital gurney for thirty-six hours straining to push that big-headed boy out from between my legs. But oh no, he was in no hurry to get out of me—it was like he was scared to come into the world!

Now he's grown and done forgot about the nine months I carried him inside of me, done forgot about what I went without so that he could have.

All that sacrifice, all that pain, and for what? Nothing, that's what! Not even a fucking phone call.

"Oh," I said.

"I miss you, baby."

Did he miss me or was that just something he felt he needed to say?

If he missed me so fucking badly, why didn't he just hop his ass on a plane and come home and show me how much he was missing me? He wasn't missing—

"What was that?" I asked, pressing the phone even closer to my ear.

Was that a woman I heard in the background? Deeka had a woman laid up in his bed, spread eagle, her cookie spread out for all of the world to see. He probably had his finger up in her right now. Son of a bitch!

"Nothing, babe, just the television. Wait a minute—let me turn it down."

Likely story! What's he doing now, sucking on it, licking it?

"There, is that better?"

I looked at the phone and calmly placed it back down on its cradle.

Fuck him.

Chevy

· · · · · · · · · ·

I was still stewing over my humiliation at Melu-Melu yesterday when my cell phone rang. The word "Unknown" came up. That could only mean one of two things: it was either Noah calling or a bill collector, and I didn't want to speak to either one of them.

I was stretched out on the couch, Anthony Hamilton blaring from the hi-fi. I turned on my side and my vision fell on the stack of bills piled on the sofa table. I quickly turned my attention to the aquarium and the expensive fish, which watched me with disdain from behind the glass.

Had I fed them today? I couldn't remember.

I turned roughly onto my back and my eyes locked with the glossy, smoldering ones of the artist formerly known as Prince as he glared down at me from the poster on the wall.

Eyes, eyes everywhere, I thought, and turned back onto my

side again. My stomach grumbled but I ignored it—there wasn't any food in the refrigerator anyway. I had thirty dollars in my wallet, but needed that to buy a Metrocard to get to work next week.

I was going to starve to death.

Maybe I could scrounge a meal off Crystal. I hadn't seen her in a while.

Sitting up and reaching for my cell phone, I rehearsed what I would say to her:

"Hey, Crystal, girl, where you been? We should really get together. It's been a while."

I grinned to myself as her phone began to ring. I had it all planned out: when we finished our meal I would dig into my purse and look up with a shocked look on my face and announce, "Omigosh, I left my wallet at home!"

"Hello?" Crystal answered with a hushed voice.

"It's Chevy—what you doing today?"

There was a pause and then she said, "I'm on the plane. We're getting ready to pull off from the gate."

I sat right up. "Where are you going?"

"Antigua. Gotta go," she said, and hung up. I just stared at the phone. Crystal was on her way to Antigua—now who would feed me?

I tossed the phone down and began to rack my brain.

There was always Geneva. I hadn't borrowed money from her in years, so she shouldn't give me too much of hard time.

Just as I was about to dial her number, the house was suddenly filled with the sound of blaring music. The base was so loud that the windows were rattling.

"What the—" I started and then rose from the couch and hurried to the window.

There was a moving truck parked in front of the house next door, and behind it were two Hummers, an H2 and H3, and an old Ford Mustang. All twelve doors were wide open, blaring the popular reggae song "Willie Bounce."

There were about eight stocking-capped men unloading the tackiest furniture I had ever seen. Mattresses with piss stains, two broken rocking chairs, and an ugly ecru-colored Formica dining table with matching chairs. "Ecck!"

Standing in the middle of the sidewalk was an oversize woman with multicolored extensions hanging from her scalp like ropes. She was dressed in a pink tube top that barely covered her triple-D-size breasts or the stomach that bulged out beneath it.

And to top it off, she had the nerve to be wearing shorts, putting her varicose veins on display.

A cigarette dangled lazily from the corner of her mouth, and gathered around her legs were more than a dozen children, ranging in age from two to eleven, not counting the infant she balanced on her hip.

I stepped back from the window and thought, Oh, Noah is going to have a fit.

I'd been desperate in the past. But not as desperate as I was sitting on the train headed uptown. Headed to Geneva's place. Headed to the projects.

I was left with no other choice. A girl's gotta eat, gotta get her hair and nails did, right?

Funny enough, as I was sitting around debating whether or not I was going to call Geneva, the phone rang and who do you think was on the other end? None other than Geneva Holliday herself!

We hardly ever call each other, so imagine my surprise.

After the obligatory hello she launched right into the fact that Crystal was off again, running behind that man, and how all men were shit to begin with, including her son.

Now, that statement took me off guard, because Geneva loved that son of hers more than life itself and I had never heard her say a negative word against him.

She went on to say that both Eric and Deeka were over in "Sadi-rabia," fucking everything that moved.

"Saudi Arabia," I corrected her, but Geneva didn't hear a word I'd said, and if she had, she just ignored me.

"It's just you and me, Chevy, just you and me—we got to stick together," she said.

Just she and I? I didn't think so.

I gave the phone a quizzical look. Geneva sounded out of her mind. "Have you been drinking?" I ventured.

"Nah, but I sure do need me a Corona or two right about now," she grumbled, and took a long puff off her Newport. "You wanna come up and knock back a few with me?"

Now, y'all know I don't drink beer, but I would if I could get a meal and few dollars out of it.

"Sure. I'll be there by two."

So here I was, seated on the A train headed uptown. I tell you, the things a woman has to do to get along in this world.

Crystal

· · · · · · · · · · · · · ·

We stopped at a rum shack that was perched on top of a hill overlooking the ocean. The heat was less suffocating there, being kept at bay by the cool ocean breeze.

I ordered a bottle of water and a vegetable patty; Neville also had a veggie patty but chose to wash his down with a bottle of beer.

We sat in silence for a while, watching the other patrons but mostly staring out over the water. I was full, spilling over with peace and happiness. I'd only just arrived, but I knew I wouldn't be near ready to leave in seven days. And, as if reading my mind, Neville reached across the small white plastic table and asked, "Can't you stay a little more than a few days?"

I smiled at him. "I wish I could, but I've taken so much time off already." I sighed and ran my thumb along the back of his hand.

"Really?" Neville's expression was one of surprise. "It's just April."

"I know—I've been in kind of a bad place," I said, moving my eyes away from his face and back out to the water.

"What's going on with you, babe?" Neville's voice was laced with concern.

"I don't know," I lied. "I think maybe I need a change."

"Well, Antigua is a great starting point."

My eyes found his face again. His strong jaw, the three gray whiskers gleaming in the midst of his otherwise dark mustache. He was beautiful.

"Yeah, I think it is."

We sat a little longer, talking some, but mostly just savoring the beauty that was thriving all around us. The sun had already started to dip when Neville guided the car up the narrow road that led to his home.

"Something's different?" I said as I stepped from the jeep.

Neville grinned proudly. "Yes, I had the outside painted."

I snapped my fingers. "That's it. Wow, it looks wonderful. What color is this?" I asked, moving closer to the side of the house.

"Vanilla."

"Vanilla." I moaned as I leaned my face close to the wall and stuck my tongue out.

Neville laughed. "I doubt it tastes like vanilla, though."

Raven, Neville's black pug, was the first to greet us when we stepped through the door. Sherman, the African gray parrot, was the second, squawking loudly from his corner in the living room and then saying, "Hello."

Even the rainbow-colored tropical fish seemed to wave their fins in welcome from within their glass aquarium.

I slipped out of my mules and left them on the straw mat at the door. The wooden floor was warm beneath my feet. Neville carried my bags into the master bedroom, while I walked to the sliding glass doors and slid them open.

The cool evening air rushed in. Below, the boats in the harbor moved slowly out to sea, while others dropped anchor and settled in for the night. All of them turned on their lights and suddenly the dark sea seemed to be filled with twinkling stars.

"God, it's so beautiful here," I said aloud.

"What's that, baby?" Neville asked, coming up behind me and wrapping his strong arms around my waist.

"I said, it's so beautiful."

Neville kissed my neck. "Yes, yes, it is. And you being here makes it even more beautiful."

I turned into him then, pressing my lips against his mouth. Our tongues found each other. His mouth was hot and he was already hard, and my hand responded by pushing its way underneath the waistband of his linen pants, finding the narrow slit in his Calvins, and then wrapping around his manhood.

"*Ooooh,*" I moaned, already feeling my legs beginning to buckle. I wrapped my fingers around his meat and marveled at how my heart and his member were beating the same rhythm.

Neville was slowly unbuttoning my blouse, and then unclasping my bra, springing my breasts free. His mouth was on my nipples; his tongue felt like hot taffy on my skin, and just as sweet. I threw my head back in ecstasy.

We were in plain sight, right on the front veranda, the moon a spotlight on our foreplay. I could hear cars moving up and down the road along the side of the house. I knew that the passengers could clearly see our prelude to lovemaking, but I didn't care.

"Come on," Neville said in a husky voice as he took hold of my hand and led me from the veranda. I thought that we were headed toward the bedroom, but instead we walked the length of the house and out through the back door.

Once outside, he pointed to a tall wooden structure that stood directly in the middle of the backyard.

"What's that?" I asked, bringing my hands up and onto my breasts. I was suddenly aware of my nakedness.

"You'll see."

I followed him to what looked like a huge wooden box. Once there, I saw that there was a black handle, which Neville pulled. The door swung out and open. I peeked inside; it was a shower.

"A shower? Outside?"

"It's great, baby—do you know what it feels like to bathe your skin with the blue sky overhead, or the stars?"

He reached in and turned the shower on. Without another word, he stripped out of his clothes and stepped in, beckoning me from beneath the spray of the water. After a moment's hesitation, I followed.

"Let me," he said, when I reached for the sea sponge on the shelf.

After he squeezed what smelled like lavender bath oil onto the sponge, he instructed me to turn around. "Press your hands against the wall, spread your legs."

I did as I was told.

Neville started at the base of my neck, with slow circular movements that released the knots I had carried in from New York living. Then he moved the sponge down my back, across my buttocks, and then gently, ever so gently, to the space between my buttocks.

My breathing went shallow. I wanted to turn around, but Neville put a firm but gentle hand on my shoulder, pushing me back into position.

When I was good and soapy, Neville leaned his naked body against me. Cupping my breasts, he rolled my nipples between his thumb and forefingers while he stroked my spine with his tongue.

I was shaking; my fingernails clawed at the wood.

Neville's penis was between my legs. I squeezed my thighs closer together. He moaned and began a slow thrust. I pushed back; I wanted him inside me so badly.

The simulation sex went on for a while, and just when I thought I wouldn't be able to take any more, he pulled away.

I waited.

He was against me again, the head of his penis poking at the round cheeks of my ass, poking, prodding, until . . .

"What the—!"

The head was in—it was in . . . Oh God, he'd entered that part of me that had been off-limits to every man I'd ever had sex with. But he was in, and . . .

And . . .

And . . .

Actually, it didn't feel half bad.

"Are you okay?"

Neville's breathing was labored; his hands gripped my hips for dear life. "You're tense."

Of course I was tense. I had never had a dick in my ass before.

"I'm fine, baby, I'm fine," I whispered, and turned my head a little, planting a slight kiss on his chin, letting him know it was okay—I was okay with it.

I pushed my hands against the wall, moved my feet farther apart, and pushed my behind into him.

"Oh, shit, baby, oh, shit." Neville groaned and inched in a bit farther.

My anus constricted.

"Damn," he muttered again. "Every part of you is as sweet as sugarcane."

I told myself to relax, just relax.

He pushed again.

"Oh God, oh God." Neville was shouting now, pushing in deeper. His grip so tight on my skin, it was painful.

He was hurting me, but the pain was mixed with pleasure. I wanted to tell him to stop—to go deeper—to pull out—to go deeper.

I squeezed my eyes shut, bent into him a bit more.

I was moaning, groaning, clawing at the wood as Neville started to stroke. It was a slow, steady in-and-out that caused Neville to howl.

"Are—are you in?" I asked breathlessly. "Are you all the way in?"

"Y-yes." Neville could hardly respond. His breath came in ragged sheets. Me, I couldn't believe I'd taken something that size up into my—

"Oh, oh, oh!" Neville began to squeal. Two more strokes and Neville's entire body went stiff for a second and then began to vibrate, as if he'd stuck his finger into an electric outlet.

When it was over, he collapsed onto my back, breathing heavily.

We were quiet, just the sound of the water beating down onto our naked bodies.

· · ·

"I have to meet a client later," Neville said after settling himself in the chaise longue beside mine. We were spending the day on the beach.

I smiled. "Oh, really?"

Neville squinted at the sun-kissed ocean before pulling his shades down over his eyes. "About seven o'clock, at the Megan."

"Dinner and dessert?" I teased, reaching for my plastic cup brimming with piña colada.

"Yeah." He laughed.

"Can I go too?"

I didn't know why, but I really wanted to see him in action.

"Ah, c'mon, Crystal, you don't want to see that."

"Yeah, I really think I do. I think it will put everything in perspective for me."

Neville's right eyebrow arched. "Perspective?"

"I mean, I know what you do. I'd just like to see it firsthand."

"You'll look at me differently."

"No, I think I'll see you more clearly."

Neville sighed, reached for the sunblock, squeezed the white liquid into his palm, and said, "Lay back, you're starting to burn."

I wore a Norma Kamali dress. It was at least ten years old, but it was a classic. The sea moss–colored linen looked breathtaking against my skin. I took a cab down ahead of Neville. I needed to get there early, to get a good spot.

I requested a seat at the front of the restaurant, which would give me the best view of the harbor, Neville, and his date.

Neville had a standard table at the Megan. It was the restaurant where he brought all of his first-timers.

The first time was the only time he would pay. After dinner and dessert (Neville à la Neville), the woman would be baited and pulled aboard and he'd never have to dig into his pocket again.

"Would you like to see the wine list?" the waiter asked me.

"Yes, please."

Neville told me that this woman, a Ms. Sonja Everett, was fifty-two years old. She was the mother of one daughter and the grandmother of three. Her husband had died three years earlier, leaving her a fortune. He'd met her on the beach a few weeks ago and she'd hired him to take her grandsons Jet Skiing and then hired him again to take the whole family for a day trip around the island on her dead husband's catamaran.

Neville knew she was interested in him; he'd caught her staring at him a number of times. Peeling his clothes off with her eyes. She'd given him a hundred-dollar tip after each hire.

I wanted to know how he knew her worth; I couldn't imagine someone offering up that type of information to a total stranger.

"People talk. She's been visiting the island for years. And I Googled her."

My eyes turned into saucers. I had no idea that being a gigolo had become so sophisticated.

The waiter returned. "Have you decided, ma'am?"

"Yes, the Pinot Grigio, please."

"Wonderful selection. Would you like to order an appetizer?"

"Not right now."

"As you wish."

Neville said that he'd engaged her in conversation; they'd shared stories about some of the same countries they'd both visited. Sonja was impressed.

"Is she good-looking?" I asked, really hoping that she was a dog.

"She's okay, I guess, for an old white woman. A nip and a tuck wouldn't hurt, but the old gal is holding up pretty well. She's got great tits."

Neville was a tit man, that's for sure. But I also knew now that he was an ass man.

I grimaced but forced a light smile. "I can't imagine that they're real . . . her tits. She's over fifty."

"No, they're not." Neville laughed. "She hugged me and it felt like cement blocks pressed against my chest."

"So how did you approach her about, you know, the date?"

"I told her that I thought she was an amazing, beautiful woman and I'd like to get to know her better and she suggested dinner, and I suggested Megan's."

"Just like that?"

"Easy as pie."

The waiter returned with my glass of wine. I sipped the sweet nectar and chuckled at the thought of what I was doing. Chevy would be shocked, but then she would be impressed. Geneva— well, who knew what she'd think about all this. We just didn't seem to be on the same page anymore. And Noah with his crazy ass would have wanted to pose as my date so he could eavesdrop too.

The maître d' was walking a patron in my direction. She was a tall Nordic-looking woman with hair the color of an eggplant. The hours in the sun had left her skin ruby-colored and speckled with brown spots. Her face was lined, not heavily, but enough so that I could see the wrinkles beneath the candlelight.

Our eyes locked and she offered me a brief smile. I returned the smile and saluted her with my wineglass.

The maître d' pulled the chair out for her. My stomach

flipped—her back would be to me, and I wanted to see her face. I almost said something, but then Sonja said, "No, I'll sit there instead," indicating the chair that would allow her to face the ocean.

After a while she turned to me and asked in her heavy Irish brogue, "Are you dining alone?"

Her question startled me. I turned and looked into her deep blue eyes.

"Yes, I am—and you?"

She smiled. It was a naughty smile. "Do you mind?" she said as she pulled a cigarette from her box of Dunhills.

"Not at all."

She lit it, inhaled deeply, and then blew a stream of smoke into the air before her. "I'm having dinner with my future husband."

I began to choke. On my saliva, on the air around me, on her words!

Sonja panicked, extinguished her cigarette, and then joined the waiter, who was patting me heavily on my back.

"Are you okay?" the waiter asked, reaching for the glass of water on my table.

I nodded my head. "Yes, yes, fine, thank you," I said gratefully as I took the water from him and carefully sipped it. The waiter waited a moment, saw that I was fine, and then moved on.

Sonja remained standing beside me.

"Are you quite sure, darling?" Her hand was on my shoulder.

"Thank you, yes."

She returned to her seat, picked up the box of Dunhills, and placed them back in her purse.

· · ·

He was late.

It was seven-thirty and Neville still had not shown up. I was on my second glass of wine and had broken down and ordered an appetizer. Sonja was checking her Rolex for the umpteenth time when Neville finally strolled in with a bouquet of birds of paradise.

He leaned in and kissed her affectionately on the cheek while simultaneously winking in my direction.

The curtain was up. It was showtime!

Geneva

. . . .

i **looked** at the clock. It was just past one when I ushered the young girl out of my apartment. I'd stuffed a five-dollar bill in her hand. "Sorry for the inconvenience," I muttered as I showed her to the door.

I'm sure she thought I'd lost my mind, calling her yesterday morning like a lunatic. She already had two heads scheduled but promised she would be here first thing Sunday morning.

First thing Sunday morning turned out to be just past one in the afternoon.

I'd already changed my mind twenty different times about my hair, and when she arrived I had decided on keeping my new do.

"Sorry," I said again as I gave her a little nudge on her shoulder, helping her over the threshold and out into the hallway.

Just as I turned the lock on the door, the phone began to ring. "Hello?"

"Chica," my coworker Darlene purred from the other end of the line. "Whatcha doing?"

"Nothing."

"I got two tickets to a Broadway show—my man gotta work, and anyway, I don't like Broadway."

"Oh."

"So I wanted to know if you'd like to go? Maybe you and your boyfriend, Dickie."

"Deeka. He's out of town."

"Oh, no. What about one of your friends?"

I started to say that I didn't have any friends. But then I remembered that Chevy was on her way up. "What time does it start?"

"Three o'clock."

I hadn't been to a play since Deeka took me to see *The Color Purple*. "Okay, why not?" I said.

"Oh, goodie, *chula*. I will leave the tickets at the box office."

"Okay, so what play is it?"

"Um, let me see. Wait a minute."

There was some rustling of papers, and then she was back. "Okay, it's called *Drama, Who Don't Got None?*"

I hadn't heard about that play.

"Which theater?"

"The Lincoln."

Chevy

· · · · · · · · · · ·

the Lincoln? Geneva, that's not Broadway!"

"Well, yes it is—it's located right on Broadway. See here?"
she said, pushing the paper she'd scrawled the address on in my
face.

I sighed. I hadn't been to the Lincoln Theater since I was a
teenager. I felt that the Lincoln Theater was a ghetto outlet for
everyone and anyone who thought they were a playwright.

I sure as shit didn't want to go.

"Geneva, it's already after two. You say it starts at three? We
don't have enough time to get there."

"Yes, we do," Geneva said, reaching for her purse. "We'll
catch a cab."

· · ·

We stepped out of the cab and onto the sidewalk. There were dozens of people milling about, mostly women ranging in age from eighteen to seventy-five and dressed in everything from "hoochie couture" to "Preach, Reverend, preach" Sunday go-to-meeting attire.

I rolled my eyes. This was going to take all the patience I could muster. Geneva and I walked over to a booth that had a piece of loose-leaf paper taped on its glass enclosure. Scrawled across the lined white sheet in black marker was TIKIT BOOF.

I winced.

The young girl behind the glass seemed to be of Asian and black descent. A female Tiger Woods. Her hair was dyed yellow, pink, and jet black and hung in choppy layers around her face. When she smiled, the blood red lipstick she wore on her lips was also tracked across her teeth.

Her left eyebrow, right nostril, and chin were pierced with silver loops, and when she said, "Thanks" after Geneva presented her benefits card as ID, I saw that her tongue was pierced as well.

As we started toward the door I was almost knocked over by a large, shiny black man dressed in a canary yellow zoot suit. I was temporarily blinded by its glaring brightness but recovered quickly enough to see that that man's wing tips and cowboy-like hat were the same color.

"Country mother—" I started.

"Hush your mouth," Geneva warned.

We stepped into the lobby and were greeted first by the smell of franks and then the scent of Smirnoff vodka. What a combination, I thought as my stomach turned over.

Directly in front of us and standing behind a little cart of liquor and plastic cups was a man I was sure I'd gone to high school with, so I quickly turned my head, lest he spread the rumor that Chevanese Cambridge had become a lifelong subscriber to Ghetto.com.

Geneva made a beeline toward the frankfurter station.

"Can I have two with everything?" Geneva began, holding up two fat fingers. "What you gonna get, Chevy?"

As hungry as I was, I wasn't about to eat one of those murder dogs. Pig snouts, rat guts, and some of everything were in those franks.

"Nothing."

We were shown to our seats by a tall, lanky boy who couldn't have been older than seventeen. He wore a black do-rag beneath a white Pirates baseball cap. I just shook my head. What was going on with the youth of today?

Geneva managed to ease her wide hips down into the small seat. It took her another five minutes to arrange the platter of food she'd carried in with her. She had changed her mind at the last minute and ordered three hot dogs along with two bags of potato chips and a large plastic cup of Pepsi.

"I'm PMSing," she whispered guiltily when she saw the disgust on my face.

"Whatever."

The MC came out, and to my astonishment it was the shiny black man in the bright yellow suit. He fed the crowd a few corny jokes in his country drawl, laughing out loud at his own wit while the stage lights clung to his gold teeth. I looked at my watch—it was after three.

"Wasn't this supposed to start at three?" I said, more to myself than to Geneva.

"*Guuuurrrl,* you know black people can't get nowhere on time." Geneva laughed as she bit down into the first hot dog.

Finally the house lights dimmed. Streams of people made

their way to their seats. The stage curtain went up just as a woman larger than Geneva settled herself down beside me. I immediately became claustrophobic.

The performers began delivering their lines, most of which I couldn't understand because the speaker system was shit.

It was obvious that the people in the first five rows didn't have a problem hearing what was going on, because they were howling with laughter. The woman beside me must have had bionic hearing, because she was shrieking with glee. Not only that, but she was saying the lines right along with the actors, like she'd seen it ten times or more.

"That's some funny shit right there!" she leaned over and screeched in my ear.

It was going to be a long afternoon.

Fifteen minutes in and Geneva was on to hot dog number three. I watched from the corner of my eye as she devoured it in two bites. I pulled my eyes away and placed them back on the stage, but nothing of interest was going on there. Just five characters snapping their fingers and twirling their heads on their necks as they spouted lines in perfect Ebonics.

I closed my eyes. I would sleep through the torture. In no time I was dreaming, about what I wasn't sure, but it was getting good when my nose was suddenly flooded with the scent of fried chicken. My eyes flew open and my head jerked left, toward the aroma. Big Mama next to me had brought in a bag of Kentucky Fried Chicken!

She pulled leg after soggy leg from that bag, chomping furiously on it until her teeth hit gristle and she began to suck.

Geneva's radar went off and she leaned forward, snatching a peek at the woman. Leaning back, she whispered from the corner of her mouth, "Now *she's* got the right idea."

Crystal

• • • • • • • • • • • • • • •

i've got to say that I was turned on and stayed turned on until Neville strolled in at three o'clock in the morning smelling like Sonja.

The dog and I was wired, so when Neville walked through the door we both popped right up.

"How was it?" I asked, my voice filled with excitement.

Neville gave me a sideways look. "You're sick, you know that?" he teased.

I ignored him. "Tell me everything."

"I will not." He laughed as he stripped out of his clothes and headed to the bathroom. Raven followed; me, I remained in bed.

When he reemerged, terry cloth towel wrapped around his waist, I was still waiting for the details. "C'mon, just the juicy parts."

"There are none." Neville yawned as he pumped the Vaseline

Intensive Care lotion into his hand and began to slather it onto his legs.

"You did have sex with her, didn't you?"

He pumped again—now he worked the cream into his arms, across his chest. "Yes, but it was horrible."

"What?" I pulled my legs up to my chest.

"She was as dry as the Sahara. We had to use a lubricant."

"You're kidding." The excitement in my voice dropped.

I was thinking about my own twat. Would it be a wasteland by the time I hit fifty?

"Does she have a nice body? She looked really toned to me."

"She was wearing a girdle," Neville said. "She's really flabby. She's had some surgery too, so there are these ugly angry-looking scars across her belly." Neville faded off and then shuddered with the memory.

"So how did you manage to . . . you know?"

He was seated on the bed now, his back to me; he was doing something with his hands. I leaned over his shoulder; he was holding his penis, stroking it.

"What are you doing?" I asked, instantly aroused, my voice heavy with lust.

His penis swelled with every stroke, and we both watched in quiet awe.

"Do you want some?"

"Oh yeah, baby, Mama wants some," I said, lying back, tossing the sheet off my naked body, and spreading my legs.

Geneva

. . . .

monday morning, I decided to take three pills.

I'd really gone overboard yesterday. The chips, hot dogs, and Pepsi-Cola at the theater and then Chevy and I went to this diner called Oswald's on Amsterdam Avenue and had cheeseburgers, vanilla shakes, and apple pie. And then I came home and had a peanut butter and jelly sandwich, which I washed down with a tall glass of milk.

So I'd slipped a little. We all do every now and again, and that's why I have these little yellow pills to help me out when I do.

As soon as I took them I started feeling better. Those pills were like an energy shot to my system. Sometimes, though—and I'll only admit this to you—I do get a little light-headed, but that's about it.

Charlie came out of her room, dressed in a pink and blue dress that was as wrinkled as I don't know what.

"What happened to your dress, Charlie?" I asked as I started toward her. It was nearly eight o'clock and I needed to drop Charlie off at school and make it to work by eight-thirty.

"I dunno," Charlie responded as she stood transfixed in front of the television.

The good feeling was leaving me. "Come here," I barked, suddenly angry at the world.

Charlie didn't flinch. I charged toward her, swooping her up and carrying her into my bedroom. She began to wail.

"Shut your mouth before I shut it for you!" I bellowed, shaking the open palm of my hand in front of her face. Charlie's mouth snapped shut, but her eyes continued to spill out salty tears.

The ironing board was a solid fixture in my bedroom. I never took it down; I just left it standing against the wall, in between the dresser and the television stand. I hurriedly pushed the plug of the iron into the outlet. Once it began to sizzle I snatched at Charlie's arm. Her eyes were filled with fear as she reached for the hem of her dress, intending to pull it off.

I slapped her hands away. "We don't have time for that."

I got to work late of course, a full thirty minutes late. Thank God my boss wasn't there. But Darlene was, and she glared at me when I rushed through the door.

"Don't say a word," I said, holding my hand up and moving swiftly past her.

I'd served at least ten customers by the time the call came in.

"Geneva, it's for you," Arthur, the fry cook, said as he held the phone out toward me.

"This is Geneva."

"Geneva, this is Eric."

I rolled my eyes at the sound of my ex-husband's voice.

"Yeah?"

"I just got a call from Charlie's school . . ."

My heart began to race. What had happened to my baby? Why did they call Eric instead of me?

"What's wrong?" I screamed.

"Calm down," he urged. "The teacher said that Charlie just started crying and then asked them to call me—"

"Crying? Is she sick, hurt—"

"No, Geneva, she's fine. Just a little shook up."

"Shook up?"

Eric's voice dropped to whisper. "Yeah—I went to get her and she told me that you yelled at her and then that you ironed her dress . . ."

I looked at the phone. Eric's voice faded in and out. Suddenly my head seemed to be filled with cotton. "What—Eric, what did you say?"

"I said, Geneva," Eric began again in a tight voice, "that Charlie told me you took a hot iron to her dress while she was still in it."

Chevy

· · · · · · · · · · · · ·

all of that torture for a horrible meal and a measly fifty dollars!

It was Monday afternoon and I was still stewing over that fiasco disguised as a play I'd attended at the Lincoln.

Geneva and the other patrons had enjoyed it to no end. And of course they had—they were as sophisticated as dung bugs—dung bugs' entire world revolved around shit!

I probably could have gotten more money out of Geneva if we'd left from the side exits and not back out through the front, because there, set right out front, was that street lit author Persistent Pablo.

Persistent Pablo, from what I'd heard, had spent eight years in the Kansas City penal system. He'd acquired his GED and had self-published his first book while serving the last six months of his sentence.

He'd found his readers in the hair and nail salons. The welfare offices and Laundromats.

When his two-year probation came to an end, his father loaned him his Nova, and Persistent Pablo, along with his boxes of hard-core street lit, set out for New York City, where he'd promptly sold over three hundred books from the trunk of his car.

Some New York publisher had zoned in on him by the time he'd self-published his fourth novel: *A Nigga Dies in Brooklyn.*

That book brought him instant fame, and now Persistent Pablo could be found in bookstores nationwide.

He didn't do book signings—well, not formal book signings inside of bookstores; he preferred to hold court on city sidewalks, and one was sure to find him and his bright red Escalade—the hood spray-painted with his likeness—along with his sales crew and hundreds of copies of the twenty or so titles he'd published, outside any event where there would be a large attendance of black folk.

"Oooooh, Persistent Pablo!" Geneva had shrieked, her hands digging into her pocketbook as she plowed through the crowd toward him.

"I read *Pussy Galore* and *Cock's Pit!*" she gushed once she was in front of Pablo. "I *looooooooooooved* them."

Tall and reed thin, Pablo looked as if he'd fallen out of the ugly tree and hit every branch on the way down.

"Thanks for da love, my shorty," he said, grinning triumphantly.

Someone please save me.

Geneva walked away with three of his ten-dollar books.

As we made our way to the diner I said, "Geneva, how can you read that garbage?" Geneva didn't even answer me—she was already devouring the words with same hungry enthusiasm she'd devoured those three franks at the Lincoln.

A soft knock came at the door, pulling me from my musings.

"Come in."

In walked LaTangie. Tan-gee.

"How y'all doing, Chevy?" she said as she swayed over to the chair and sat down before I could object. "You all had a good weekend?" she continued when all I did was glare at her.

"How can I help you?" My tone was firm, professional.

She was unfazed by my rudeness.

"Well, Anja wanted me to stop in to make sure that you'd received the invitations for the Holloway party on Wednesday."

Yes, I had received the invitations. Which were really more like four gold tickets to the hottest social party in Brooklyn.

Taking place in the halls of the Brooklyn Museum and at twenty-five thousand dollars a head, the Holloway party was the benefit event of the season, if you were a Brooklynite.

This year the funds raised would go to the renovation of a ten-story apartment building that had been abandoned by its owners some twenty years ago. The city had taken it over and the Ain't I A Woman Foundation had purchased it for a song. The foundation intended to turn it into a shelter for single mothers and children—all of whom had been diagnosed with the AIDS virus.

"Why?" I asked.

"Well," LaTangie began, twirling her red hair around her index finger and cocking her head childishly to one side, "Anja wants me to collect them and bring them to her."

Why didn't Anja just call and ask me to bring them to her?

My eyes held LaTangie's as I picked up the phone and pressed the speed dial that would connect me to Anja. The call immediately went into voice mail, but I pretended that she answered.

"Anja, Chevy here . . . What? Yes, she's sitting right here. I thought it best that I deliver the invitations to you directly because we need to discuss a few things, if that's okay with you? Yes, okay, see you in five."

I hung up the phone. LaTangie's doe eyes stretched to saucers.

"I'll bring them to her," I said with a smug smile. "You can go back to whatever it is you do."

LaTangie's face remained sweet as she rose from the chair. "Okay then, Chevy, you all have a nice day," she said as she turned and exited my office.

I wasn't sure, but I believe I heard the word "bitch" float to me on the back draft of the closing door.

Geneva

· · · · · · · · · · · · · ·

I was on the bus home soon after I hung up the phone.

To tell you the truth, I couldn't remember much of what had happened that morning. I do remember ironing Charlie's dress, but I sure don't remember her being in it. The morning was a blur and that wasn't unusual—most of my mornings were a blur. I was always running late, always in a rush.

Eric had taken Charlie to the movies and he would meet me back at my place. I wasn't looking forward to that: I knew he was angry even though he'd tried hard to keep his voice low, his words civil.

The bus swerved, just missing a pizza deliveryman on a bicycle but sending me careening into the lap of a passenger. The man, a white male, was red with embarrassment—I'd crushed his *New York Times* and his Dunkin' Donut. "Sorry," I muttered as I pulled myself back to my feet.

I could hear snickering from some of the other passengers. I dropped my eyes in shame and got off at the next stop, which left me ten blocks from home.

"Where the f—" Eric started but then stopped. Charlie stood beside him, clutching his hand. "Where have you been?"

"What? I left work as soon as you called me," I said, not ready to meet my daughter's accusing eyes.

"Geneva," Eric began, his tone impatient, "that was two hours ago."

I blinked. Two hours? I looked at my watch; it was one o'clock. I didn't have an answer to Eric's question, so I just looked down at Charlie and said, "You feeling better, baby?"

Charlie nodded her head, but her eyes were wounded. I sighed, my heart breaking into a million pieces. "Mommy's sorry for yelling at you this morning. You know sometimes Mommy gets—

" 'Tressed," Charlie said.

"Yes." I grinned. "Sometimes mommy gets stressed." I reached out to her, planting my hand on her head. "Do you forgive me?"

Charlie nodded again. Releasing her father's hand, she took tiny steps until she was at my side.

I looked up at Eric. His eyes were fuming.

"You know," he spoke through clenched teeth, "if she'd told her teacher what you'd done, the school would have called child protective services on you."

"She's making it up," I said. She had to be. Why would I do something like that to my child? "You know she has a wild imagination. She probably just didn't want to be in school today."

Eric's face registered doubt—in who or what I wasn't sure—but nevertheless, his eyes softened. "Hey, sweetie," he said, easing down to one knee and coming eye level with Charlie. "I'll see you next week, okay?" Eric tweaked Charlie's nose and then hugged her.

"Okay, Eric," Charlie said. Charlie had never warmed to calling him Daddy.

Once we were in the apartment, I tried to remember what had happened between the time I'd left the diner and my arrival at the apartment. I remembered falling on the man and then getting off the bus and walking home. It couldn't have taken me that long to cover ten blocks—or maybe it had?

Oh, well—I had so much on my mind, maybe I'd just kind of dazed out and my body went on autopilot.

And this thing with Charlie—she had to have been lying. Children told lies all the time, even the dangerous types that could get a parent placed behind bars. I'd have to talk to her about that. Not today, though, but soon.

May

Crystal

·····················

i **was not happy** to be back in New York.

I'd only been home for three weeks, but it felt like a year. I'd returned to a shitload of paperwork, e-mails, and meetings that took up most of my day. On top of that, I had to attend the gala event at the Brooklyn Museum, something that I truly did not want to do. I just didn't have it in me to put on an evening dress and my happy face.

I so wanted to be back in Antigua, barefoot and braless, sitting on Neville's veranda and staring out at the sea.

When I arrived home my answering machine was filled with messages. One from Chevy advising me that she would see me at the gala, two from my mother, ten from Geneva, who with each message sounded like a different person—I was beginning to think that she was bipolar—and one from Noah saying he was flying in on Friday, May 26. I wasn't to tell Chevy, because he wanted to surprise her.

I refocused my attention on the task at hand. Somehow over the past few years, my job description had changed from schmoozing to crunching numbers. I squinted at the columns and columns of digits and, as I could have predicted, my head began to hurt.

I opened my desk drawer and pulled out the bottle of Tylenol I kept there for just these moments. After popping two pills, I washed them down with a bottle of Fiji water. I made a mental note to call the optometrist in the morning. These sudden headaches were becoming more frequent.

I leaned back in my chair and waited for the medicine to take effect. Just as the pain was starting to ebb from my temples, the phone rang.

"Crystal Atkins."

"Chrissy?" Peyton, my mother, questioned from the other end of the line.

"Hi, Mom, how are you?"

"I'm fine, sweetie, how are you?"

"Fine."

"You don't sound fine. You sound stressed."

"That too. Just a headache. What's up?"

My mother was silent for a while; I suspected she was carefully choosing her words. We'd spoken just once since I'd returned, and that conversation had been brief.

"Oh, nothing—I was just thinking about you and wanted to hear your voice," she said.

I knew she really wanted to hear the details of my trip, but I wasn't telling.

"Thanks, Mom. Glad to know you care," I said drily.

"Of course I do, honey. Listen, I thought maybe if you could get a few days off you could come out and visit with me?"

Now, she knew I'd just gotten back from Antigua. "I can't take any more time until July."

"Well, how about I come and visit you?"

Don't get me wrong, I love my mother, but I just wasn't in the mood to have her in my space for an extended period of time. She had a bad habit of rearranging my things, going through my drawers, and wanting to talk—in explicit detail—about my sex life.

"Um, Mom, I'm really up against it here at work, and now is just not a good time. Let me get back to you with a date."

"Oh, I understand." She was wounded; I could hear it in her voice.

"But hey, Memorial Day weekend is next week. Maybe I can get a cheap flight out then," I said, even though I knew I wouldn't even try.

"Yeah, baby, that would be nice," Peyton said, her voice light. "Okay, honey, the girls just pulled up."

"Oh, where are you all off to?"

"Bingo, and then later, target practice."

"Target practice, with guns?"

"Yes, sweetie."

"Why do you need to know how to shoot a gun, Mom?"

"Hey, a girl has to know how to protect herself," Peyton said, and then, "Ta-ta, sweetie—remember, Mommy loves you."

And with that she was gone.

I placed the phone back down onto the base. That mother of mine had a better social life than I did.

It was just past eight o'clock, and from the looks of things I would be here for at least another two or three hours.

I looked down at the pages before me and the pain in my head started its thumping once more.

The ringing telephone pulled me from my slumber. I looked at the clock and it said it was just past midnight.

I was annoyed—the first time the phone rang, it was around eleven. I was so tired, all I could do was pull the pillow over my head—I told myself that whoever it was would just have to leave a message.

Now it was ringing again. I gave in and answered.

"H-hello?" My voice was hoarse, so I cleared my throat and tried again. "Hello?"

"Crystal?" My name came out as if the person calling it was in a tunnel.

"Y-yes. Who's this?" I asked, pulling myself into a sitting position and stifling a yawn.

"It's Neville."

This was a spot of sunshine on an otherwise gray week. I brightened.

"Neville! How are you?" I squealed, suddenly no longer tired. "Make me jealous—tell me about the beautiful warm days and crystal clear waters." I laughed, pulling my knees up to my chin.

"Baby, how beautiful can it be when you're so far away?" Neville responded in that sexy Antiguan accent that never failed to make me wet.

I grinned; he was a man who knew how to make a woman feel like a woman.

"It's so nice to hear from you, Neville. What's going on?" I asked, straining to hear Antigua's night sounds.

"Not a thing, girl. How are you?" Neville asked, and his tone shook a bit, as if he knew that I was going through something. I felt the tears begin to well up in my eyes, but I blinked them away and turned up the cheer level in my voice.

"Just working hard. Nothing new, same old thing."

"Ah, you sure?"

I looked at the phone. Neville was perceptive, but this was ridiculous.

"Yes, of course. Why, did you have a dream about me or something?"

"Gal, I'm always dreaming about you."

"Oh, Neville," I gushed.

"When are you coming back down to see me?"

I wanted to say *I'll be right there, today, the last flight in.* But I had to be realistic: my life, my real life, was right here in New York.

"Oh, I hope I can get down there in the next few months or so. I just need for things at work to calm down."

Beep.

The tone sounded, advising us that our call was about to come to an end.

"Hey, Crystal, I only had a few dollars left on this phone card. I'll give you a call again—"

Your call has come to an end. Thank you for using Caribbean Way Phone Cards.

I listened to the computerized voice, and then when it was done I listened to the dial tone.

Geneva

· · · · · · · · · · · · · ·

the apartment was clean. Spic and Span clean.

Charlie was fast asleep in her bed, a bottle of champagne was chilling in the fridge, and Teddy Pendergrass was crooning from my boom box.

Everything was perfect.

Deeka and Eric were flying in tonight. Their plane was due to land at eight-fifteen, and it was just past nine. Deeka was coming straight here; Eric was shooting over to the apartment he shared with his girlfriend.

Deeka and I would have all night to get reacquainted.

I'd changed my lingerie six times, starting with a red teddy that had the crotch cut out and moving to an all-over ivory-colored piece that had the tits cut out. Then I'd changed my mind yet again and donned a scallop-laced emerald green number that showed all that God has blessed me with, but I didn't think that Deeka could handle all those blessings on his first night back.

So I finally decided on a simple white silk spaghetti-strapped nightie.

At ten o'clock he still hadn't arrived. I tried his cell phone, but it went straight to voice mail. Stretching out on the couch, I decided I would channel surf to pass the time.

When I found my eyelids were beginning to droop from sleep, I sat up and turned on some bumping music—that would keep me awake—but after ten minutes of Mobb Deep, all I had was a headache.

I would call Crystal. Yeah, that's what I'd do, and we'd talk until Deeka got there. But when I dialed her number all I got was her answering machine.

It was almost eleven o'clock at night. Where the hell was she? Shit, where was my man?

. . . Were they together?

When I opened my eyes the sun was up. The clock on the cable box told me it was just after seven in the morning. I'd spent the entire night on the couch . . . alone. Deeka had never shown up, and he hadn't even called.

I turned my head. Ah, just great, my neck was stiff! Slowly I eased myself erect and rolled my head on my neck—a lot of help that was. All it did was make the pain worse.

"Good morning, sleepyhead." The familiar voice came from across the room. I slowly turned my head to see Deeka seated in the old recliner, wrapped in the patchwork quilt I'd owned for ages.

I blinked; surely my eyes were playing tricks on me.

"Deeka?"

"Yeah, 'Neva, it's me."

Stiff neck forgotten, I was up and on him in a flash.

"Oh, baby, I missed you so much, when did you get in, why didn't you wake me . . ." I spoke a mile a minute while covering his face in kisses.

"Slow down, babe, slow down." Deeka laughed, pulling me into his lap. "I got here about four this morning, I tried to wake you, but you were out cold."

"Oh, baby, baby, I'm sorry. Why didn't you go and get in the bed?"

"I haven't seen you in a month, babe, I just wanted to sit here and watch you sleep."

I blushed. Was this a man, or was this a man!

He reached up and touched my hair. "You cut it," he said.

My heart seized up. He hated it.

"I like it, baby. It really suits you."

Like I said, what a man!

"You wanna go, um, lay down together?" Deeka's tone dropped to a seductive level as he nodded toward the bedroom.

I giggled but didn't move.

"C'mon," he urged, his penis already growing hard beneath my thigh.

We had to act quickly—I had a six-year-old that would be up in a few minutes!

"What's the hurry, Geneva?" Deeka cried as I ripped at his clothes like a wild woman. We needed to get naked, and fast.

"Charlie," I said, pulling my nightgown over my head.

"Oh yeah," Deeka said, and dove into the bed.

Tossing the nightgown to the floor, I dove in beside him. We turned toward each other, our foreheads bumping loudly.

"Ow!"

"Sorry, baby."

"Me too."

We kissed, hungrily, and our hands moved over each other's body, stroking, massaging, pulling.

"I want to be on top," I said breathlessly, already moving into position.

"O-okay."

I dropped one breast into Deeka's open mouth. He sucked happily on my nipple, while I twirled his nipples between my thumb and forefinger.

I was propped up on his belly; I could feel his cock throbbing between my legs.

"Put it in," he begged. "Put it in now."

I eased up, grabbed his meat, and slipped it inside of me. It had been so long, I almost exploded on contact, but I controlled myself and grabbed hold of the headboard and began to ride.

"I'm going to fuck the shit out of you!" I warned, as I bit down on my bottom lip.

"Fuck me, baby, fuck me!" Deeka cried, his hands gripping my hips.

The bed bucked wildly up and down with our frenzied rhythm. The headboard banged loudly against the wall and I felt the pleasure begin to swell in the pit of my stomach. Deeka's eyes were tightly shut and his mouth hung open as if he were in the middle of a forgotten statement.

The pleasure, hot and prickly, moved through my entire body, bringing me to the most fucking fantastic orgasm I'd ever had!

"I'm *cccccccccooooooooooooommmmmmmmmmmmming*!" I screamed as all my womanly juices exploded inside me and drained down onto Deeka's dick.

Deeka shuddered, his teeth clamping together as the muscles of his face strained beneath his skin.

"Whooooooooooooooooh," he breathed, after shooting his load. "Damn, baby, that shit was bananas."

I rolled off him and onto the bed. We were both soaking wet with perspiration.

"Yeah, it was," I said, still trying to catch my breath.

"Mommy?" Charlie's voice floated over to me from the doorway.

Horrified, Deeka and I scrambled to cover ourselves with the sheet.

"Hey, hey, baby—go on back to your room. Mommy's coming," I said, smiling and shooing her with my hand.

Charlie rubbed one eye while she peered at us with the other and said, "Why did Deeka have his pee-pee in your kitty-cat, Mommy?"

Noah

· · · · · · · · · ·

It felt damn good being back home again!

Brooklyn, New York, had a vibe that London just did not have.

When the yellow cab came to a stop in front of my beautiful brownstone, I felt my heart leap in my chest.

"What the hell?" I shouted. The front steps were littered with supermarket circulars, making my home sweet home look like an abandoned dwelling.

Furious, I tossed a ten and a twenty at the driver, snatched my Louis Vuitton luggage from the trunk, and marched up the stone steps.

I'd been nice enough to allow my friend—soon to be ex-friend—Chevy to live in my home while I cohabited with my partner in London. And as meager as the rent I charged her was, most of the time I had to hunt her down for it.

No telling how many times the light and telephone had been cut off since she'd been living here. Chevy had her priorities all fucked up.

I set my luggage down in front of the mahogany double doors. I would pick up the circulars first and then head inside to see what damage had been done there.

There had to be at least thirty circulars on my steps. I couldn't believe Chevy had allowed them to pile up so!

"Is that Noah!"

I froze for a moment, wishing that I had left the step cleaning till later, because now I was going to have to answer the million and one questions my nosy neighbor was going to sling my way.

I took a deep breath, put a smile on my face, and slowly turned around.

"Yeah, it's me, Sharon."

Sharon was a tall, lanky seventy-year-old woman who had lived on Stuyvesant Avenue her entire life. Literally. She was born in the brownstone she still lived in. She'd seen the neighborhood go from good to bad and back to good again.

"Noah!" she screamed, rushing me and throwing her wiry arms around my neck. For being close to a century old, she sure was quick on her feet. "It's so good to see you!"

"You too."

"Let me help you with that, baby," Sharon said as she reached for some of the circulars and started toward the garbage can that sat alongside the steps.

"I just hate these things. They make such a mess of the block," she slurred through her gums. Sharon had a habit of forgetting to put her partial plates in her mouth. Sometimes she'd remember to slip in the upper plate and not the lower one, or vice versa. Today she'd forgotten the lower partial, so her bottom lip had rolled in over the bare gum, making her look ten years older than she was.

"So how you been?" she asked, folding her arms across her sagging breasts. She'd stopped wearing bras back in the sixties, when they were burning them.

Now, I knew that she didn't really care how I was doing but was just being polite to ask, and I started to answer because I knew that as soon as I got started she was just going to cut me off.

"Well, I'm doing—"

"That's good—now let me tell you about this new family that done moved in next door to you." Sharon leaned in and began whispering in a conspiratorial tone. "Gotta be about fifty of them."

"Fifty? That many?" I teased; Sharon had a habit of speaking in hyperbole.

"Yeah, big house, four stories, like mine. Not like yours, only three," she huffed. I felt myself stiffen. There was some type of weird hierarchy where brownstones were concerned: if you had a four-story brownstone, you were in a higher class than the three-story brownstoners.

"White?"

I had to ask, the neighborhood seemed to be getting lighter with each passing day.

"Colored," Miss Sharon said.

I started to ask her how many colors they were, but it would have gone right over her head. She was born during the time when we were considered colored. She'd never moved beyond that to black, or the most recent term, African American.

"Oh, really," I murmured, and shook my head. "Okay, Miss Sharon—look, I got to get on in the house and unpack," I said, already starting up the steps. "It was nice seeing you again," I threw over my shoulder.

"Yeah, okay then," Miss Sharon said, and started out of the gate before turning around and asking, "Noah, you still a faggot?"

I had corrected Miss Sharon on that term more times than I could count. She'd used it on me so much that I had become desensitized to it. And really and truly, she didn't mean any harm.

I turned around, offered her my warmest smile, and said, "Yes, Miss Sharon, I am still gay."

She nodded her head thoughtfully before offering me her best piece of advice: "Take it to the Lord, Noah. He can fix it."

"I will remember that, Miss Sharon. Thank you," I said before pushing the key into the lock.

The inside of my house looked like who did it and why! The garbage can in the kitchen was running over with trash. There were dishes in my stainless-steel sink and dried egg stuck on the grates of my Amana stovetop.

My hardwood floors didn't look like they'd had a damp mop dragged across them in months, there was dust on everything, and all of my tropical fish were floating belly-up in the tank!

I just stood in the middle of the living room, staring open-mouthed at the disorder and dirt. I wanted to scream, but it caught in my throat. I want to move, but my feet were cement blocks.

I couldn't imagine what it looked like upstairs.

How could one person be so irresponsible? So filthy? So fucking inconsiderate with another person's home?

Well, I tell you this right now, that bitch was out of my house. Out, out, out!

After standing there for a few minutes I finally felt the feeling coming back to my feet. Before I would do anything, I needed to calm myself down—shake off the jet lag and talk myself out of killing Chevy. Turning toward the kitchen, I tried my best to avert my eyes from the floating fish. Once in the kitchen, I forced myself not to puke as I donned my rubber gloves and opened the dishwasher. I would simply put all of the filthy dishes in the dishwasher. That's what it was there for, right? Well, to my surprise, there were already dishes inside. I pulled the rack out, intent on putting the clean dishes away, but to my further surprise and mounting disgust, the dishes inside were dirty. Not just dirty, but grimy. There was mold growing on the fucking dishes! Do you hear what I'm saying? MOLD!

I slammed the door to the dishwasher and decided that this was as good a time as any to venture upstairs and see what damage had been done there.

Before I even hit the top landing, I could hear the toilet running. I barged into the bathroom and shook the silver handle, then turned to see that the faucet was dripping. I tightened the hot water handle and then the cold and the dripping stopped. The tub itself had a ring so dark around it that I knew I was going to have to use a power hose to get it clean again.

Steaming, I moved from the bathroom into the back bedroom that was supposed to be Chevy's room. There were mountains of clothes thrown across the bed, burying it from view. Shoes lay strewn across the floor, covering the once glistening hardwood the way moss covers a sidewalk. The smaller room beside it doubled as a walk-in closet and a place to store the ironing board. The closet doors were open, and inside there were dozens more of Chevy's clothes and shoes. Across the ironing board were crumpled towels, towels that I suspected had been used and then thrown carelessly across the board instead of being deposited in the hamper.

I turned on my Birkenstock heels and moved down the narrow hall toward my bedroom. I braced myself and closed my eyes before I stepped inside. I stood there for a minute before opening one eye and then the next. It was as I thought it would be. A mess!

That bitch had been sleeping in my bed. From where I was standing I could see coffee stains on my ecru-colored raw silk duvet. The fucking coffee cup, still filled with coffee, was sitting on the nightstand. Fashion magazines everywhere—some open and dog-eared, others stacked in haphazard piles along the wall.

My head was spinning and then my eyes fell on the pièce de résistance—a lime green thong that Ms. Chevy had just apparently stepped her stank ass out of and left in the middle of the floor.

That nasty heifer!

Chevy

. . . .

geneva, if you call me one more time to tell me about your fucking dinner, I ain't coming!" I said, and snapped my cell phone closed.

I leaned back into my office chair and cussed softly under my breath. That damn Geneva had called and e-mailed me about a hundred times about the party she had planned for Saturday, which was tomorrow.

How many times does a sister need to be reminded?

Besides, I had other shit on my mind. Shit like LaTangie.

I saw her in the dining room today, sitting at Anja's special table. I've been working for Anja for more than a year now and I have never seen her in the dining room.

Her table was like a damn shrine—separated off by red velvet ropes. The kitchen staff changed the flowers and tablecloth on a daily basis. And those employees who had never met Anja, or who were so infatuated with her that they thought of her as a goddess, could often be found standing near the velvet ropes, their eyes glazed as they used their cell phones to snap pictures of the table Anja never used.

I didn't frequent the dining room—shit, I couldn't afford it—but I popped in to get a five-dollar cup of yogurt and was caught off guard by the sound of Anja's husky laughter.

When I looked up, LaTangie and Anja were clinking champagne glasses.

I stood there in a daze for a long moment. I was fucking Anja and had never been invited to the "table."

Now, I wasn't in love or no shit like that, but I had become accustomed to the fucking, and as I watched the two of them carrying on as if they'd known each other for years, I began to feel as if the arrival of LaTangie somehow meant the departure of Chevy.

The sight of them ate at me all day long, and when I left work it was all I could do not to pull out my cell phone, call Miss Anja up, and cuss her out.

But that would be the actions of a strung-out bitch, and I am not one.

So I just let it be for the weekend. I would tackle Ms. Anja on Monday.

For now, I had to get in back to Brooklyn and get Noah's house in order. Geneva slipped up and told me that he was flying in from London in the morning, so I still had plenty of time.

.   .   .

I knew something was wrong as soon as I pushed the door open, because the scent that hit me was the fragrant bouquet of red currant candles.

Damn, I thought to myself as I began to pull the door shut again, Noah's home.

Noah

• • • • • • • • • •

the last time I hit a woman I was fifteen years old and
Sheniqua Jenkins had mushed me in the face because I was
sporting a Wave Nouveau and she was still walking around with
that tired, drippy-ass Jheri curl that had eaten her hairline to
nothing.

And here I was now, on the brink of forty, getting ready to
fuck Ms. Drama up!

I'd spotted her just as she was backing out of the doorway and
caught her by the opening of her blouse, yanking her narrow ass
back into the house. My intention was to hit her like a woman;
an open-palm smack right across that funny valentine–looking
face of hers. But she beat me to the punch and brought that crocheted pocketbook she carried down onto my head.

I don't know what the fuck she had in that bag, but it felt like
a paperweight and I saw stars.

After that, it was on!

I balled up my fist and swung, but that Chevy was quick and ducked it before I could make impact. We tussled with each other into the living room, where I managed to throw her down onto the couch. I had her pinned, but she was fighting like a wildcat, and I had to jump off her because she was trying to claw my face!

"Bitch, are you crazy!" I yelled when I was finally able to catch my breath. Chevy had her fingers arched, ready to swipe. One leg was planted on the floor, the other dangled in midair, bent at the knee, poised to strike.

She looked like one of the characters straight out of *Crouching Tiger, Hidden Dragon*.

"Are *you* crazy!" she hollered back.

I spread my arms out at my sides. "Look at my house, Chevy— just look at it. How could you let my home come to this?"

Chevy's mouth opened and then closed. That bitch had no excuse.

I pointed to my fish tank. "That's two thousand dollars' worth of dead fish, Chevy!"

Chevy's eyes rolled toward the tank and then back to me. She remained quiet.

Her silence just further infuriated me, and I took a quick step forward, ready to pounce again. Her leg came out and the sole of her shoe connected with my stomach. I went flying backward into the wall. My head made contact with the glass of my framed *Purple Rain* movie poster.

CRACK!

Before I could recover, Chevy was up and out the door, her weave flying in the wind.

"And don't come back, bitch!" I yelled as she double-timed it down the street.

Geneva

* * * * * * * * * * * * * * *

i hadn't expected to get Noah on the phone. For some reason I thought he was coming in the next day.

I just wanted to leave him a reminder message about the party, so imagine my surprise when I heard Noah's British-tinged "Hello?"

"Noah?"

"Yeah."

"It's me, Geneva."

"Hey." Noah sounded stressed.

"Um, is everything okay?"

"Now that that bitch is out my house it is."

"Chevy moved out?"

"No, she ran out. We had a fight."

Well, it was bound to happen.

"A fight? Are you serious, Noah?"

"As serious as a heart attack," Noah huffed. "I don't want her back in this house. I don't want her back on this block!" he screeched. He sounded close to tears.

I truly didn't know what to say, so I just said, "Well, okay, don't forget about the party—"

Before I could finish my sentence, Noah slammed the phone down.

Whatever Chevy had done this time, it must have been bad.

I dialed Crystal's number. It was just past seven and she should have been home from work for at least an hour.

"Hello?" Crystal's voice was groggy.

"Crystal, are you sleeping?"

"I was."

"Didn't you work today?"

"No."

"Are you sick?"

"Sick and tired," she mumbled.

"What?"

"No, just tired and needed a day off."

Well, it seemed to me she'd been taking off plenty of days.

"Oh, um—have you heard from Chevy?"

"No," Crystal began in a bored tone. "What she do now?"

"Well, I don't know, but I just spoke to Noah and he says that they had a fight."

"I'm surprised it took so long."

"Are you sure you're okay?" I ventured again.

"Yeah, just tired. I'll call you back later."

"No need. Just don't forget that the party starts at—"

I heard a soft click and then the dial tone followed. I had been hung up on twice in less than ten minutes. What the hell was going on?

Chevy

· · · · · · · · · · · · ·

Once I got on the street and down the block and around the corner and still didn't see any signs of Noah behind me, I knew I was safe.

I looked a mess. Noah had ripped the entire front of my blouse, so my beaded La Perla bra was on show.

Two young men made vulgar gestures with their crotch as I hobbled along, clutching the material closed. I had broken the heel of my left shoe in my haste to escape, and to make things worse, Noah had pulled my hair so hard that now one of my tracks was hanging.

Damn him and his overblown temper. Had he been truthful about his arrival date, none of this would have happened. I would have had the house spic and span by the time he sashayed his faggot ass through the door.

Of course, the fish would have still been dead.

I knew him, though. He was all mush in the middle, so I figured it would be safe to return in the morning. He'd be calm by then, and I could finagle my way back into his good graces and his home. But for tonight, I needed a place to stay.

I thought briefly about walking down to the Akwaaba Mansion, Bedford Stuyvesant's black-owned bed-and-breakfast, renting a room, and chilling there. But that would cost me. I needed to crash somewhere for free.

I racked my brain for a minute. I could call Crystal, but I certainly wasn't in the mood for a lecture.

Geneva wasn't an option. There was no way I was sleeping on her ratty couch in her tacky apartment, in the projects, no less.

Then it hit me; I had the key to Anja's Upper East Side apartment.

It was Friday night, and as far as I knew Anja was spending the weekend at her home in Connecticut, leaving the apartment free and clear for me to use.

I started toward the train station.

Tomorrow would be a better day, and all this drama would be over.

I was sitting on the A train, feeling real good about myself, when I was suddenly accosted by a stench so powerful, I felt as if I had been slapped. My head jerked on my neck and my hand came instinctively up to cover my nose.

Slowly, my eyes rolled to the left. There beside me stood a bum, a homeless person, a sanitarium refugee left over from the Rockefeller release program!

He was dressed in a moth-eaten orange and gray plaid woman's coat complete with rat fur cuffs and collar—and he was grinning down at me.

His hair was a matted mixture of Afro and dreadlocks, complete with bits of lint and ragtag yellow ribbon.

"Hello," he said, sneering.

My mouth fell open and then snapped closed again. I took a quick inventory of the car, and from what I could see there were no empty seats available, so I slid closer to the person next to me.

"Oh, you gonna act like you don't hear me talking to you?"

I felt laughter building in my throat and coughed, trying desperately to clear away the giggle.

I chanced a glance at the face again. His expression was stone-cold mean, and my eyes dropped back down to my lap. I was beginning to shake.

"Don't ignore me. I'm a person too, you know," he jeered, showering me with spittle.

That was it for me.

"Get the fuck away from me," I hissed, pressing my hip bone deeper into the one of the man next to me, who promptly closed his *Da Vinci Code* paperback, stood, and walked away.

Oh, shit!

The bum seized the opportunity and settled himself down beside me. He gingerly crossed his legs, carefully shaking the lapels of his beaten coat and patting what I was sure was lice-ridden hair. I shook my head in disgust and wondered why it was fucked-up things always seemed to happen to me.

My fear was slowly being replaced with anger, and what I really wanted to do was cuss that man from head to toe and then take my pocketbook and slap him across the head with it a few times. He was a big man, but I was quick and agile and curious to see if those Tae Bo classes would pay off.

"Okay, what the hell is your problem!" I turned and shouted into his face.

I had to pull the crazy card before he did.

The man's eyes popped in his head and then narrowed. "Problem? I have no problem. It seems you're the one with a problem. I said hello to you, and you were too rude to respond."

A woman, two men, and a teenage girl all stood in unison and walked toward the front of the car.

"I don't know who the hell you are, but I'm warning you, I have Mace!" I shrieked and began rifling through my pocketbook. In truth all I had were keys, half a pack of chewing gum, a compact, lipstick, comb, cell phone, and wallet.

In a flash, the bum snatched the bag from my hands, turned it over, and dumped the contents. I was stunned as I watched my stuff slide across the filthy floor.

"Things! Things—that's all you people care about!" he bellowed.

I turned astonished eyes back onto the man. A litany of cuss words coated my tongue, but I was so angry that all that would come out were gurgling sounds.

"All I wanted was a hello! I'm not garbage, you know—I'm a real person, with real feelings!" he wailed, beating his fists dramatically against his chest. "Just a hello, is that too much to ask?"

I abruptly stood, careful not to turn my back to him as I stooped to collect my belongings.

"I used to have a home, a family, friends," he ranted on, "and then my job was downsized, I lost my apartment and my family . . . Ohhhhhhh, in just three months I was living on the street!"

I walked away from him, down toward the conductor's booth. I willed the train to move at the speed of light. I needed to get away from this maniac.

"You!" he bellowed pointing a filthy finger at me. "You too could end up like me—hungry, displaced . . . just wanting a hello!"

"Not me!" I screamed back at him as we pulled into the station and the doors parted.

I stormed into the building, right past the shocked doorman.

"Um, miss. 'Scuse me, miss!" he cried as he took off behind me, finally catching up with me at the bank of elevators.

"What?" I snarled, my hands on my hips. "What, you don't know me now"—I zoned on his name tag—"Carl?"

Carl watched me with a stupid look on his face. It was clear he wasn't the sharpest knife in the drawer. "I'm Anja's assistant, Chevy," I said as I jabbed impatiently at the elevator button.

Carl pressed his index finger thoughtfully against his chin. "Um . . ."

"Um, nothing, Carl. Go away," I ordered, waving him away with my fingers.

When the elevator door opened, I nearly knocked over two female teenagers, iPod earphones coming out their heads like millennium-issued appendages. I bullied my way into the elevator before they could step off. "Bitch," they shouted after me over their shoulders. "Your mama," I replied as the door began to slowly close.

All I wanted to do was take a hot shower and crawl into bed.

The elevator door creaked open and I stepped out onto the sixth floor.

I pushed the key into the lock and turned, but nothing happened. I pulled the key from the lock and examined it. Yep, this was the right one, the only red key I had on my key ring.

I inserted it again and tried to turn it in the other direction, but nothing happened.

I stood there staring blankly at the black door for a minute, trying to comprehend what was happening. After two more tries, I had to accept the truth.

Anja had changed the fucking lock!

I knew this had something to do with LaTangie, I just knew it.

I stormed out of the building, flipping the bird to the grinning doorman as I went.

I didn't have any money—well, not enough for a hotel—so I stormed down the street, attempting to walk off my anger.

It would be a while before the realization hit me that I had no place to go.

Noah

....

it was nearly midnight when I finally got my house back to
normal. The dead fish had been placed in plastic bags and
thrown out into the garbage. My floors were swept and mopped
clean, the linens on my bed changed, and I had even found the
strength to Hefty-bag all of Chevy's belongings.

After pouring a glass of wine, I dimmed the lights in my living room, put on my Syleena Johnson CD, and sat down on the
couch, propping up my feet on my leather ottoman.

I was home.

Just as I was beginning to completely relax, the thumping
bass of Kanye West and Jamie Foxx's "Gold Digger" began to
pound through my walls.

I was annoyed but figured the song was coming from one of
those black Yukons the neighborhood drug dealers drove up and
down the streets in.

I told myself, This too shall pass. But it didn't. It just kept coming. My windows were shaking, the framed photographs on my walls were rattling, car alarms were going off and my temper was about to follow.

Jumping up from the couch, I ran to the front door, swung it open, and stepped outside. My head turned left and then right, and that's when I saw the problem.

My new neighbors had set up six-foot-high speakers in their yard. There were four teenagers sitting on the front steps and five children playing tag around the speakers.

My other neighbors had come out to look too. But not one said a word. They just shook their heads in disgust and retreated back behind their doors.

After a moment, a large black woman emerged from the house, dressed in a pink bra top and denim miniskirt. She looked like a poster child for bad taste. She had no business dressing like that. I laughed into my hand, guessing that she weighed three hundred pounds.

Around her neck she wore at least eight different gold chains, each holding three or more charms. The gold was cheap, I could tell from where I stood. I had an eye for precious metals.

She had a slew of gold bangles on each wrist, and they made an annoying chinking sound when she raised her arm to guzzle the forty she gripped in her fat hand.

"Hey, neighbor!" she turned and hollered at me.

I brought my hand up to block the glare; the top front row of her teeth was encased in platinum.

Geneva

· · · · · · · · · · · · · · · ·

Yes, we'd finally been busted by my six-year-old. Deeka still couldn't look Charlie in the eye, even though I'd explained to him a million times that Charlie was still just a child and wasn't quite sure what it was she witnessed.

But Deeka kept saying, " 'Neva, she asked you why my pee-pee was in your kitty!"

I told Charlie that she'd seen wrong and that Deeka and I was just playing a game of horsey.

When she asked why we were naked, I told her that we'd gotten really hot and so took our clothes off.

When she asked if she could play next time . . . I just sent her to her room.

I don't think she's traumatized by what she saw; in fact, I think she's already forgotten all about it.

But just to be safe, tonight I sent Charlie down to my

mother's house so that we could get as wild and as loud as we wanted to.

We'd been watching *Lackawanna Blues* for the second time, and when I looked over at Deeka, he was nodding.

I nudged him in his side. "Deeka, wake up."

Deeka's eyelids fluttered, and he wiped at the spittle that was forming in the corners of his mouth. "I'm sorry, baby." He yawned, reaching for his glass of Pepsi, which had gone warm an hour ago. "I'm just beat."

I knew he was and tried not to complain, but damn. He'd walked through the door, pecked me on the cheek, and handed me the bag of Popeyes chicken before flopping onto the couch, pushing his hand down into the waistband of his pants, and fixing his gaze on the television. Before long he was out cold, leaving me, the two drumsticks, biscuits, and the container of coleslaw all alone.

"I saved you a drumstick, baby," I said, wiping frantically at the grease around my mouth. I wanted so much to be ravaged by him tonight.

"Nah, you go ahead and have it. I'm so tired I can't even chew."

The alarms went off inside my head. If he was too tired to chew, then he was certainly too tired to do anything else. I nudged him again.

"Is Mr. Peter tired too?" I said coyly as my hand slipped into his lap and then up to his crotch.

Deeka grunted, smiled, and then politely moved my hand. "Yeah, I think so."

I huffed. Is this what my life had turned into? A Friday night in front of the television with a Corona and a bag of chicken?

Shit, I'd had that life before Deeka came along.

"How come we don't go out anymore?" I whined.

Deeka opened one bloodshot eye. "Don't start, 'Neva," he warned.

I folded my arms like a two-year-old. "Why?" I demanded.

"Geneva, you know I'm still trying to catch up on my rest. Do you think that month on the road was easy? It was tiring."

I pouted.

"Stop being so dramatic," he said as he stood up, stretched, and started toward the bathroom, where he proceeded to take a loud piss with the door open.

We were like an old married couple. Where had all the romance gone?

"Can't you close the goddamn door!" I bellowed, and then grabbed the remaining drumstick and took a huge bite out of it.

Deeka reemerged, pulling up his zipper.

"Wash your hands, Nasty," I ordered without looking at him.

"You keep talking to me like I'm one of your children," Deeka chastised, and walked back into the bathroom, where he washed his hands. Returning to his seat beside me, he tried to pacify me by laying his head in my lap.

"Get off," I said, thumping his head with my forefinger and thumb.

"Oh, it's like that, huh?" Deeka turned and looked up at me.

"Yeah, it's like that, Negro," I retorted.

Deeka sighed, rolled his eyes, and sat up. "So do you want me to leave?"

Of course I didn't want him to leave, but my mouth said, "Do what you want. I don't care."

I was really regressing.

"Are you about to be on the rag or something?"

"Fuck you," I shouted, and shoved his head off my lap. In a split second I was on my feet and across the floor.

Deeka sat on the couch, shaking his head in amazement.

"I'm out, girl," he mumbled and pulled his six-foot frame to a standing position. "I'll see you tomorrow."

I watched him walk to the door and put his hand on the knob. He threw one last look over his shoulder that said *Last chance* . . .

I sucked my teeth and turned my head away.

Geneva

....

Okay, so Christmas in May might seem like a strange concept to some, but to me it's not.

You see, last Christmas, Deeka and my son, Eric Junior, had to go out of town to perform. And when I say out of town, I mean *waaaaaaaay* out of town. To South Africa, to be exact.

To make things worse, not even my girls were around to celebrate with me. Crystal was in Antigua with Neville, and Chevy was in the south of France with her boss, Anja.

And Noah was skiing in Switzerland with his lover, Zahn. Even my mother went out of town.

Leaving Charlie and me no other choice but to spend Christmas with my crazy family in Queens.

If it wasn't for Charlie, I would have been content sitting in front of the television with a Pop-Tart and a pint of Ben and Jerry's.

So when Noah called last month and said he would be spending the summer in New York, I got the unique idea of celebrating Christmas all over again with my nearest and dearest. Of course I wanted it to be a surprise, so I just told Deeka and the rest of them that I was cooking a welcome home dinner for Noah.

Won't they be surprised when they come through the door and see my artificial tree decked out in all its Christmas flair!

I've hung silver and gold tinsel everywhere, and I even have plastic mistletoe dangling from a piece of dental floss I tacked to the ceiling.

Outside it may be seventy-three degrees, but in apartment 6C, it's Christmas!

Eric Senior called just as I finished basting the turkey, mixing the ingredients for the stuffing, and skinning the yams for baking. Crystal had promised to make the potato salad, and Deeka was going to Brooklyn to pick up a strawberry cheesecake from Junior's.

There wasn't going to be ham because over the past year everyone I knew had given up pork except me. I guess I could forgo the swine this one time.

I had just lit a Newport (I was down to a half a pack a day) when the phone rang.

Eric Senior and I exchanged greetings and I was even contemplating inviting him over when he took a deep breath and lowered the bomb.

I just stood there for a long moment, staring at the phone like it was some kind of foreign object. I could hear his voice coming from the earpiece, calling my name over and over again, but I couldn't seem to find the will to answer him.

The sound of a car backfiring outside my window jolted me back to life and I pressed the phone against my ear and asked, "What the fuck did you say?"

Eric sighed and repeated his question: "Would it be okay if I take Charlie with Jamie and me down to Florida?"

Jamie was wife number four for Eric Senior, and Eric was husband number three for her.

Jamie Amelia Lopez, a Cuban Dominican woman, was a good eight years older than Eric, and, believe me, it showed. I could tell that at one time in her life she was a striking woman, but now her face, which was almost always made up like a Hollywood starlet's, was beginning to crease.

I knew Botox would be the natural next step for her.

But even as her face failed her, her body seemed to get younger and tighter.

Jamie went to the gym religiously, ate plenty of green vegetables, and drank gallons of water.

I suspect she's had a breast lift, because I didn't know any women who'd birthed and breastfed five children, and not to mention were knocking on fifty's door, with tits like hers.

Come to think of it, I didn't know too many twenty-year-olds with tits like hers!

Don't get me wrong: I like Jamie, but I didn't know if I liked her enough to send my baby girl on a trip with her and a father who'd only recently started to take a real interest in his daughter.

"Um, I don't think so," I stated, pressing my fist into my thick hip and rolling my head on my neck. "Over my dead body," I added.

Eric sighed. "Geneva, I am her father. I should be able to take my daughter on vacation."

"Mama's baby, Daddy's maybe," I spat.

"Stop it, Geneva. You're being unreasonable."

In the background I could hear Jamie whisper, "What did she say? It's okay, yes?"

I could just imagine her, dressed in her tight black spandex capris, stilettos, and tube top. She was a grandmother, for goodness' sake!

"Let me talk to her," Jamie demanded, and then there was scuffle, a few refusals from Eric, and finally Jamie's voice with its heavy Latin accent saying, "Hello, Geneva, how are you?" Which came out sounding like *How ark jew?*

"I'm fine, Jamie, and you?"

I sweetened my tone. I hated that I liked her. After Eric proposed marriage, she had demanded to meet me. I was a little apprehensive; none of his other wives ever showed any interest in me or the son Eric and I had together, so this was a new one on me.

We met at McDonald's. She greeted me with a large hug and began to tell me how beautiful I was and then looked around at Eric and asked what the hell was wrong with him, letting go such a beautiful woman?

I didn't know what to expect, but I certainly didn't expect that. And as I ate a Big Mac and fries, I actually felt myself starting to slip into some sort of weird adoration for Jamie.

She was so jovial and carefree. Someone that I thought could be a real good friend if she weren't married to my ex.

"I'm good. Look, Geneva, we want to take the baby with us to Florida for the summer. Eric is retiring next month, you know, and we have the house in Miami, and it would be good for her to be able to go to the beach. You know, fresh air, fresh food."

I just blinked. "What?" I coughed; Eric hadn't said anything about Charlie staying for the "entire" summer.

Jamie rattled on as if I'd said nothing.

"I told Eric to invite you too. Why not—we are all family, *sí*?"

Jamie was on some Demi Moore–Bruce Willis–Ashton Kutcher shit.

"That's very nice of you, Jamie, but I can't get away—"

"Oh, no, maybe next time. But Charlie, she can come, *sí*?"

This woman had just invited me on vacation with her family and my ex-husband, even though she knew my history with Eric. I mean, I got pregnant with Charlie while he was married to his last wife. Neither one of us were angels! Wasn't she concerned that a small flame still burned? Didn't she think that maybe a little hanky-panky could happen while she was on the beach, sunning her forty-four double-Ds?

Either she was crazy or real confident. Maybe she was a little bit of both. I caved.

"*Sí*, she can go," I said.

Crystal

．．．．．．．．．．．．

I guess Adolph Fisher was wrong about me being premenopausal, because I was PMSing like a son of a bitch!

I could see that it was going to be a salty month; I was already
craving peanuts, potato chips, and french fries. Last month had
been a sweet month and I'd gobbled down Heath bars and ice
cream like they were going out of style.

I leaned in closer to the mirror. The two new pimples were
growing in size.

I plucked up a tube of MAC lip gloss and quickly applied the
copper-colored gloss to my lips. My hand hesitated a moment
over the tube of mascara but then just came up and smoothed
back my hair. I didn't even have the strength to style my hair, so
I would be sporting a ponytail today; it was just Geneva's house,
just the gang.

I yawned loudly. I was so tired, so goddamn tired.

Oscar the doorman tipped his hat and said, "Have a good day, Ms. Atkins."

I smiled and wished him the same.

The day was warm, the sky clear, and the streets were bustling with people. I felt my spirits lift a bit. With every step, I felt lighter, happier.

I was actually smiling by the time I reached the corner and still smiling when someone from behind called my name.

Spinning around, I came face-to-face with my past, and my smile and good mood dropped away just like that.

Noah

· · · · · · · · · · ·

Saturday afternoon found me standing on the Utica Avenue station platform. I had just missed the A train, but the announcer on the busted speaker advised passengers that a C train was just five minutes away.

My mind was pondering my Zahn situation. I was missing him desperately. I missed his warm body against mine at night when we slept. I missed his corny jokes and how he tugged at the loose flesh beneath his neck whenever he was pondering something.

I missed the sex. Lawd, how I missed the sex!

The night before I was scheduled to leave, I believe we had the best sex ever. It was angry, urgent, and raw!

We sucked each other off and then I bent over and let him have me. He'd never felt so big inside of me. I was biting so hard on the pillow that I left a hole in the material.

Just thinking about it was getting me hot, and that combined with the warmth of the subway station got me to perspiring.

I shook off the memory and concentrated on the dark tunnel. I saw no indication that a train was anywhere near.

"Noah?"

I turned around. "Will!" I yelped with surprise.

Will Somers was an old flame who I'd had some trouble getting over.

We embraced and I allowed my fingers to roll across his muscled back. He still had his football player's physique, and as we separated, I realized he'd also maintained his boyish good looks.

"Hey, long time," I said, genuinely glad to see him.

"Yeah, last time we saw each other was in London, wasn't it?"

"Yes, yes, it was." I smiled as the memory floated back to me. I'd been visiting with Zahn and had decided to take a morning stroll, after which I popped into a small café and was enjoying the morning paper and a cup of tea when I looked up and Will was standing over me.

I had been astonished to see him so many miles away from New York, but that wouldn't be the last surprise of that meeting.

Will announced that he was getting married the very next day. Imagine my surprise: I had had that man's cock in my mouth just twelve months earlier, and now he'd gone and switched teams.

But it gets better—just as I was trying to digest the wedding information, his wife-to-be walked in.

Merriwether Beacon, a woman that I'd had relations with during the summer I lost my mind and started sleeping with women.

Thank God for my therapy group, Homosexuals with Heterosexual Tendencies: they saved my life and put me back on the homosexual track.

I chanced a quick glance at Will's left hand. There wasn't a wedding band there, unless that aquamarine stone wrapped in silver twine was it.

"So how are things?" I ventured, hoping he would bring up the wife before I did.

"Oh, same ole thing. But tell me, are you living here in Brooklyn or in London?"

I unfolded my life in London for Will, but as I did I was also checking him out. He didn't look like any heterosexual husband I knew. For instance, his eyebrows were very well groomed—not just groomed but waxed so thin, they almost looked drawn on. And was that lip gloss? And while yes, many straight men as well as gay men wore earrings in both lobes, how many wore gold chandelier-shaped danglers?

My eyes continued to travel . . . down.

The gray T-shirt he wore was cropped and fit his torso like a glove. I could make out every cut of his chiseled physique through the slinky thin material.

His navel was pierced, and below that was a tattoo, some statement in Latin. On his feet he wore pink suede Timberlands that laced up to the knee.

I stopped talking right then and there and abruptly asked, "What the hell is going on with you?"

"What?" Will said, blinking stupidly.

"Last time I saw you, you were Mr. Macho, Mr. I'm Taking a Wife. So what's this?" I said, indicating the pink lace-ups with one hand and the belly ring with the other.

"Oh, this." Will giggled girlishly and waved his hand at me. "The marriage didn't work out."

"Can I guess why?" I asked sarcastically.

Will just nodded his head and murmured, "Uh-*hmmmmm*."

"Damn."

"Oh, please, honey child, it's not like she didn't know what she was getting."

My eyes popped. "She knew?"

"Of course she did. She met me at a gay club, for God's sake!"

"Langston's?"

"The very same. But listen, Noah, it's funny that I'm running into you like this, 'cause she has really been wanting to contact you."

"She? Merriwether? For what?" I said, already having flashbacks of the three-hour fuckfest we'd had some years earlier.

"I don't know. I didn't have a number or anything to pass on to her, so I just told her to scout the hangouts and maybe she'd bump into you."

I took Will in once more; I just couldn't believe what he'd turned into.

"Anyway, you got a cell phone with you? I'll give you her number and you can lock it in, call her if you want to. I won't say I saw you if you don't. Cool?"

"Cool."

After I'd punched in Merriwether's number, I asked, "So how long did it last?"

"Shit, less than three months, and good thing too, she'd started eating like a pig and got fat as a cow!"

My jaw dropped. "What?"

"You heard me," Will said as he fished a compact from his front pocket. Flipping it open, he checked his glossy lips. I watched in quiet amazement.

After he was done primping he turned to me, rolled his eyes seductively down my body, leaned back on one leg and asked, "So you free or what?"

I looked at Will like he'd lost his mind. "No, I'm in a relationship," I said, balking beneath the thundering sound of the approaching train.

Crystal

· · · · · · · · · · · · · ·

I was still in a daze when I arrived in front of Geneva's building. Deeka was just walking up. "Hey!" he called out to me.

I offered him a weak "Hey yourself."

"You okay, Crystal?"

I wasn't okay.

"Yeah, yeah, just wondering if I turned the oven off," I lied.

"Oh, you better go back and check, then."

"No, no, I'm sure I did," I said, and forced a smile. "So how was your trip?"

"It was exhausting, but worth it."

"That's good." The muscles in my face began to quiver. Holding a phony smile is no easy task.

"You look wonderful as always." Deeka beamed. "Have you been on a beach somewhere? You're glowing."

"Huh?" I didn't hear a word he'd said.

"I said, you been away? You've got a wicked tan."

"Thanks," I piped, my hand coming up to touch my face. "I was in Antigua, but that was last month."

"Oh."

We stood there smiling at each other for a while. I liked Deeka, but we hadn't really gotten a chance to get to know one another. We'd been in each other's company a few times, but he was either coming in when I was leaving or vice versa.

Just when I felt like the silence was a moment too long, Deeka took me by the elbow and led me away from the building into the center of the courtyard.

"Hey, Crystal, it must be fate that we showed up at the same time, because I've been wanting to talk to you."

Deeka's face was suddenly a mask of seriousness.

I folded my arms in preparation for what he was about to share with me.

"Really," I breathed, bracing myself. I had no idea where this was going.

"Well, you see," he began nervously as he shot a look up at Geneva's window. "I, um, want to . . . well, I think I'd l-like to," he stammered.

I was really getting nervous now. All sorts of thoughts were running through my head. The main one was that he was trying to tell me he was going to break up with Geneva.

"Yes," I said, my voice tight.

Deeka took a deep breath, exhaled, and then said very quickly, "I want to propose to Geneva."

My face went slack. I couldn't believe what I'd just heard.

"Crystal?"

I was trying to recover, but I couldn't catch hold of the words that were swirling in my mouth. Deeka took a step toward me.

"I said I want to ask Geneva to marry me." He spoke slowly, deliberately, as though I had a learning disability.

It still took me a few moments to find my voice, and then all that came out was a whisper: "Oh my God."

I must not have been smiling, and I have to admit that my tone carried more apprehension than joy, because concern bloomed in Deeka's eyes.

"Aren't you happy for us?" he asked in a quiet voice.

"Why, of course I am. I think I'm just in shock is all," I said, and then forced a smile. I pressed one hand against my heart and used the other to dramatically swipe my brow. "Whew—I didn't know what you were going to say." I laughed.

Deeka's face darkened. "What did you think I was going to say?"

I didn't want to share those thoughts with him, so I just stepped in and gave him a tight hug and quick kiss on the cheek. "I am so happy for the two of you. Really, I am!"

And I was happy for them. Geneva was my girl, my ace boon coon, and she had found her knight in shining armor. I was overjoyed for them . . . I just felt sad for myself.

When I stepped back, my eyes were brimming with tears.

"Are you okay?" Deeka asked, resting a comforting hand on my shoulder.

"Yes, of course. These are tears of joy," I lied, my voice quaking. "So are you going to pop the question today?"

"No, no, not today. That's what I wanted to talk to you about. I want to make it real special."

I nodded as I dabbed at my eyes.

"I'd like to ask her with you and all of her closest friends and family around."

I nodded again.

"So maybe we can put our heads together and come up with something?" Deeka's eyes were pleading.

"Of course we can. Of course we can," I responded as we turned and started back toward the building.

Geneva

. . . .

everything was done. My turkey was a golden brown, my sweet potatoes were baked to perfection, my fried corn was glistening, my biscuits were moist and just the right color.

Everything was set out on the table, and I'd left a spot for the potato salad that Crystal was supposed to bring.

I reached for the pack of Newports that I kept on the top of the fridge.

I leaned over the sink and pushed the window up, blowing a long stream of smoke into the air.

My eyes picked over the few people who moved through the courtyard and settled on a couple engaged in what looked to be a very intimate conversation.

They were standing close, probably lovers, I thought to myself as I took another puff of my cigarette.

The woman stepped forward and embraced the man. They held each other for a while. I smiled and thought, How sweet.

There were a few more words shared, and then the couple linked hands, turned, and started toward the building, their faces coming into full view.

I choked. It was Crystal and Deeka!

Hurriedly I turned the faucet on and filled a glass with water. As I gulped it down, my mind kept replaying the scene I'd just witnessed. Surely there was some explanation, some reasonable explanation for them to have been standing so close . . . to have been holding hands.

Of course there was, I told myself as I filled the glass yet again.

Crystal was my girl, my best friend, and Deeka was my man. They wouldn't . . .

Or would she? Maybe Crystal hadn't really gone to Antigua. Maybe she was with Deeka. Maybe she was the one I heard in the background of his hotel room when he claimed it was just the television.

That bitch!

"Stop it, Geneva," I shouted out to the walls. Stop this insanity right this minute, I thought. You have been watching entirely too much of Maury Povich!

Deeka and Crystal were not getting it on. They both loved me, and besides, Crystal wouldn't do something like that to me, her best friend. Or would she?

My mind whirled.

Crystal had been doing quite a lot of things that were unusual to her character, hadn't she?

Well, yes, there was last summer, when she went to one of

those sex parties and slept with strangers. There was that, I mused.

And what about Neville? What about him—he was nothing but a man-whore, a "he-bitch," and she'd fucked him, hadn't she? Had even paid good money for plane tickets, flying back and forth to be with him—hadn't she?

She was unscrupulous where it came to sex, wasn't she?

Unscrupulous? I didn't even know the meaning of that word. "Shut up!" I shouted, squeezing my eyes shut and pressing my palms against my ears. When I finally did open my eyes, Charlie was standing in front of me, clutching her Pooh Bear, watching me strangely. "Mommy, what's wrong?"

I forced a smile and swiped at the cracker crumbs on her chin, "Nothing, baby. Mommy is just getting a headache."

And by that time I was.

A knock came at the door, and I swung it open to find Deeka and Crystal waiting on the other side.

I scrutinized them for a moment.

"Well, can we come in?" Deeka asked, already stepping around me.

I'm not sure, but I think I sneered at Crystal and then pretended to sneeze.

"You okay, girl?" Crystal asked.

I smirked and rubbed at my nose. "Fine."

Crystal

· · · · · · · · · · · · · ·

I almost fell over when I stepped into the apartment and saw that it was decked out for Christmas. There was tinsel, and smiling, red-cheeked Santas everywhere. To tell the truth, it was a bit nauseating.

"You hear from Chevy?" I asked as I settled myself down onto the couch and pulled Charlie into my lap. Deeka took a seat on the other end of the couch and promptly reached for the remote control.

"No."

Geneva's response was sharp, and Deeka and I exchanged looks.

"I wonder if she's going to show up today?"

"I doubt it," Geneva threw over her shoulder as she busied herself at the sink. "Not after Noah tossed her out on the street like he did."

"On the street? Chevanese Cambridge? I don't think so," I laughed. "Chevy is too resourceful to be sleeping on a park bench somewhere. She's probably laid up in one of Manhattan's top hotels right now."

Geneva grunted but said nothing.

Switching the subject, I said, "Hey, girl, the apartment looks out of this world."

And I meant that literally.

"It must have taken you days to put this all together."

Geneva was standing by the table now, folding and unfolding napkins. She shot me a look and then her eyes swung to Deeka, who was staring intently at the baseball highlights on the television screen.

"No, it didn't take me any time at all."

"Christmas in May, wow," I muttered sarcastically under my breath. "Cool."

The tension was thick between us, and I didn't know why it was there at all. Just when I was about to utter another word, a knock came at the door. I hoped it was Noah, and I hoped he'd brought a knife.

I let go a sigh of relief when Noah bounded through the door, a boxed cheesecake in hand. He gave Geneva a tight one-armed hug, then walked over and planted kisses first on Charlie's cheek and then on mine. He turned to Deeka and offered him his hand. "Hey, man, great to see you again."

Deeka stood and he and Noah bumped shoulders before patting each other heartily on the back.

"Same here, man," Deeka said.

"Let me get that from you, Noah," Geneva said, reaching for the cheesecake. That's when Noah spotted the Christmas tree in the corner of the room and his mouth fell open. "What the hell—" he started, but stopped as he took in all the other holiday decorations, then doubled over with laughter.

"What the hell is this?" he exclaimed, whirling around to look at Geneva.

Geneva's face lit up, the first time she'd smiled since I'd walked through the door.

"It's for you, Noah, because we missed last Christmas together!" Geneva squealed.

I cocked my head. Hadn't we all missed being together last Christmas?

Noah tossed his head back in glee. "Get outta here, Miss Girl. You did all this for little old me?" he cried, wrapping his arms around Geneva. "You are too much!"

"Yeah," Deeka said, walking over to the table. "She nearly worried me to death about this. Do you know how difficult it is to find Christmas decorations in May?" He laughed as he picked up the knife and began poking at the turkey.

"Well, Miss Girl, you have certainly outdone yourself. Everything looks wonderful," Noah spewed as his eyes moved over the food.

"Um, wait a minute." Noah's good mood was quickly melting away. "Where the hell is the potato salad?"

Geneva shot me a pointed look, folded her arms, and asked in a nasty tone, "Yeah, Crystal, where is it?"

Why was Geneva acting so bitchy toward me?

"Oh, damn." I slapped my hand against my forehead. "I walked right out and left it on the counter."

"Oh, well, you better hurry yourself right back home and get it. I can't have Christmas dinner without potato salad," Noah exclaimed, shaking his finger in my face.

"I, uh, I," I stammered. I didn't want to go back home. *He* might still be out there. I wasn't going back, at least not by myself.

"Noah, do you wanna come back with me?"

Noah's eyes bulged. "Not really."

"What are you, eight years old? You need someone to hold your hand while you cross the street?" Geneva spat.

She was really plucking my last nerve.

"Why don't you just admit it, Crystal?"

"Admit what?" I said, whirling on her.

"Admit that you didn't make the goddamn potato salad," Geneva snapped, bringing her hands down hard on the kitchen table.

The room went quiet for a minute as we all exchanged quiet glances.

"Are you on the rag or something?" Noah spoke very slowly.

"Or something," Deeka mumbled under his breath.

Geneva glared at him, shook her head in dismay, and then calmly turned around, walked into her bedroom, and softly closed the door behind her.

"I'm sorry," Deeka apologized. "Ever since I've been back she's been acting strange," he said, heading toward the bedroom.

"Yeah, I've noticed that too," I said, starting behind Deeka. But he held his hand up and I stopped in my tracks. I had to remind myself that he was her man, her mate, her confidant . . . her friend. He would take care of her.

I stepped back and settled myself down onto the couch.

Noah stood up and began to help himself to the food. "Merry fucking Christmas." He snickered.

Chevy

· · · · · · · · · · · ·

by the time I emerged from the subway, it was just after two in the afternoon. I'd been riding the train all night, all morning, and a good part of the afternoon. I would have probably still been on the train if not for the hunger pangs and the urge to piss.

I found a Starbucks and used the restroom, splashing some water on my face, and then ordered a muffin and Grande Decaf.

Who knew how long I'd been sitting at the table lost in my own worries.

It must have been a long time, because when I happened to look up, I saw that the staff behind the counter was giving me a strange look.

I didn't need to be asked any questions, so I gathered myself and walked to the next Starbucks. It wasn't far, there seemed to be one on every corner.

By the time I hit Starbucks number four, it was almost ten o'clock in the evening. I had twenty dollars left in my wallet and a pint-size attendant hovering over me with a Windex bottle.

I took that as my cue that it was time to leave.

I walked two blocks to a McDonald's. The schedule on the door said that closing time was one a.m.

I ordered a Big Mac, large fries, and a Diet Coke and settled myself in a corner booth.

I don't remember falling asleep, but the meaty finger of the store manager poking into my elbow was what jolted me awake.

"What, where . . . ?" I mumbled, looking stupidly around me.

"We're closing, miss," he advised me through clenched teeth.

One o'clock had certainly come quick.

I gathered my purse and rose—as elegantly as possible—from my seat. I didn't even bother to return my tray. Two steps toward the door and my bladder opened up. I spun around and started toward the door beside the registers marked BATH-ROOM.

"Hey, I said we're closing," the manager shouted at me.

I ignored him, reached the door, grabbed hold of the knob, and pushed. And pushed. And pushed again.

I was kicking and banging the door when the manager grabbed me by my elbow.

"Are you deaf or just stupid?" he said as he dragged me toward the exit.

"I just have to pee," I pleaded, already feeling my panties going damp.

"Well, then," he said, smirking as he snatched the door open, "you should have thought of that when you left your tray on the table."

And with a shove I was on the sidewalk, my hands between

my legs as I hopped from one foot to the other, trying my best not to piss on myself.

There was nowhere for me to relieve myself. All of the restaurants on the block were closed. I turned off Broadway and down Sixty-fifth Street.

It was a residential block, so it was quiet and the lighting wasn't as glaring as it was on Broadway.

Having no other choice, I ducked between a parked Honda Prelude and BMW X5, pulled down my pants, and pissed.

Panties damp, I roamed the streets for a while, trying to figure out just what it was I was going to do. The temperature was dropping and dropping fast, and all I had on was a cropped denim jacket, a thin orange T-shirt that said I'M WHAT WILLIS IS TAKING ABOUT, a pair of denim capris, and open-toed wedged mules.

I paused beneath a street lamp, pulled my compact from my purse, and checked my face—I knew it, my lips were turning blue. If I didn't find someplace warm and soon, I was going to die from hypothermia!

I looked left and then right. I had no clue where I was. I'd been walking aimlessly for hours, and my watch told me it was after three in the morning. I moved on, passing an American Apparel store and then a Foot Locker. The area was starting to look familiar. A Gap store sat on the corner ahead of me. I snapped my fingers in triumph. I was in the East Village!

My pace quickened and in a few more steps I was standing in front of the Astor Place train station. Fishing my Metrocard out of my back pocket, I hurried down the steps and through the turnstile. The number 6 train was just pulling into the station.

Jumping on, habit took over and I looked frantically around for a seat, but the train car was empty except for two people.

The whole world was home: cozy, warm, and asleep.

I sat under a poster that pictured a homeless person, with a caption that read GIVE IN THE RIGHT PLACES.

Leaning my head back, I allowed the warmth of the subway car to penetrate my skin. I had never felt more grateful in my entire life.

It looked like I would have to spend another twenty-four hours riding the train, but this would be the last time.

Monday was just a day away, and I had a huge office, in-suite bathroom, and fresh clothes waiting in my coat closet.

I would slip into the building early, shower, and change, and no one would be the wiser.

After that, I planned to go down to Accounting and get an advance on my check—just in case Noah was still upset and I needed to crash at a hotel for a few days.

Yes, I had it all planned out.

Everything would be just fine.

Crystal

. . . .

I didn't want to leave, but when ten o'clock rolled around and Noah started looking at his watch and Deeka began looking at his, I thought that, yeah, it was time to go.

After Geneva retired to her bedroom in a huff, the rest of us decided that there was no sense in wasting all that good food, and so the celebration continued on without her.

I gave Charlie a kiss on her cheek and gave Deeka a hug. "Hey, you're trembling," he said. I pulled away from him.

"Am I? I think I might be coming down with something," I lied, starting quickly toward the door.

"I'll give you a call next week," Deeka said.

"Okay."

"Hey, man, it was nice seeing you," Noah said, extending his hand.

"Same here," Deeka replied as they shook.

"Don't worry, Miss Geneva is just probably going through menopause or something," Noah joked.

Deeka just shrugged his shoulders and pulled the door open.

Arms linked, Noah and I started across Columbus Avenue toward Central Park. "I'm so glad you're home, Noah."

"Me too."

We hadn't really had a conversation, what with Geneva's episode and Charlie dominating our time by singing every song she'd learned since preschool.

But there was something else too. After the scare I'd had, my mind was floating, but Noah seemed just as occupied and I didn't feel like it had anything at all to do with Chevy.

"You okay?" I asked.

"Me? Sure, why?"

"You seemed a little distant tonight."

"I think you're confusing me with you."

Okay, so whatever was going on in Noah's life, he wasn't quite ready to talk about it. I completely understood.

"I'm fine." I laughed and unlinked my arm from his. Skipping a few paces ahead, I stretched my arms out by my sides and yelled, "It's spring and all is right with the world!"

And the Oscar goes to . . .

Noah walked me to my door, and as much as I tried, I couldn't get him to come upstairs. I really didn't want to be alone tonight.

"Nah, Miss Thing, maybe next weekend we can do the slumber party thing," Noah said, looking up at the sky. "But tonight, I'm sleeping in my own bed."

"Okay."

I didn't even try to hide my disappointment.

"Don't be giving me those puppy-dog eyes. That only works on straight men," he chastised before hugging me tight.

"Call me when you get home so that I know you're safe, okay?"

Noah blew me a kiss over his shoulder. "Will do."

This was one time I was happy that there were cameras in the hallways and elevators. That was one civil right I was more than happy to give up if it meant keeping me safe from the likes of Kendrick Greene.

I didn't know he was out of jail. And there wouldn't be any reason for me to know, as I'd stopped communicating with him the day he flooded my apartment, stole my jewelry, and was arrested on national television in connection with some drug bust.

He'd written me dozens of letters from jail, telling me how much he loved me. He'd apologized profusely for what he'd done to me.

I read every line of every letter, but I never wrote back.

He had humiliated me, stolen from me, and lied to me—but worst of all he had broken my heart.

I'd worked hard at trying to put him out of my mind, and finally I'd succeeded. So I almost had a coronary when I turned to the voice that called my name and my eyes locked with the ones of Kendrick Greene.

"Crystal."

He was propped up against a black Cabriolet convertible, dressed in a pair of jeans, brown loafers, and a white T-shirt that said DREAM.

When I just stood there staring, he pressed his palm against his chest.

"It's me, Kendrick."

I knew who the hell he was; I was just caught in a state of disbelief. He was still as handsome as I remembered. He'd put on some weight, but it looked good on him.

"H-hi," I croaked, and took a step backward.

Kendrick looked around nervously. He didn't seem to know what to say.

"Where do I begin?"

You begin at the beginning, right?

Kendrick took another step toward me. I didn't move. I couldn't move.

"I guess it would sound real cliché to tell you that I've changed, but I have."

I could smell his cologne. It smelled good. It smelled damn good. I felt myself begin to swoon. God, after all of these years, this man still had power over me.

"I spent three years in that federal prison trying to figure out how I would make it up to you when I was released. I got out on December sixteenth, and it took me from that day till now to gather up enough confidence to come here."

I waited.

"To tell you the truth, I still don't know how to make it up to you, but I figure maybe I can start by taking you to dinner."

Dinner?

"What do you say?" Kendrick's voice was warm, soft, pleading.

What do I say to that? Let's see, you move into my apartment under the pretense of the possibility of marriage, and then when you get settled in you stop working, which leads to you asking me for money—which I gave you—but apparently that wasn't enough, because you begin to steal from me to support the drug habit that I am oblivious about.

You stop bathing, yet I come home to a flooded apartment because you left the water running in the bathtub, leaving me with thousands of dollars in damages.

And then I watch the evening news to see my man—my boyfriend—the high-profile investment banker that I had planned to marry and start a family with—being hauled out of an apartment in handcuffs.

Later, I find out that you have assaulted your female drug pusher and tried to escape with her product—product with a street value of more than three hundred thousand dollars.

But because you are the son of Aldridge Greene and the heir to Greene Investments, an investment company that has been a constant on the Fortune 500 list, because of all of that, you get a tap on the wrist: three years jail time and ten years probation.

You practically ruined my life—and now here you are, proposing to fix all that with a meal?

That's what I should have said, but instead I said, "I don't think it's a good idea," and stepped around him and started quickly down the street.

"I'm going to keep coming back until you talk to me, Crystal," he said as I hurried away. "I love you!"

I was sprinting by then.

Now here I was, lying in bed, replaying his words in my head and all the good times we had together.

I curled my arms around myself and was instantly reminded of his touch and how he felt inside of me.

I flipped over onto my side and forced myself to conjure up all the bad feelings he'd left me with. I made a mental list, two columns—good and bad—and somehow, I don't know, the good column seemed to go on for miles.

Geneva

. . . .

by the time I came out of the bedroom everybody was gone except Deeka, who was slumped over on the couch, snoring. Charlie was also asleep, stretched out beside him, one arm wrapped around Pooh Bear.

I walked over and turned the television off and then lifted Charlie up and took her to bed. When I returned, Deeka was awake and stretching his arms above his head.

"You feeling better, Geneva?"

I felt ashamed. I'd planned the perfect day and then I'd gone and ruined it.

I went and sat beside my man.

"I don't know what's wrong with me. I don't know why I behaved that way."

Deeka wrapped his arm around my shoulder and pulled me to him.

"Do you think maybe you should see somebody about it?"

I snapped away from him. "See somebody like who? A shrink?"

Deeka nodded his head and reached for me again, but I shirked away.

"Do you think I'm crazy?"

"I didn't say that—"

"Well, what are you saying!"

"I just think that if you're having these wild mood swings, something has to be wrong, and maybe you should—"

I jumped up from the couch. "That's what they told my uncle Albert, they said, 'You're depressed, go talk to somebody about it,' and he did, and you know what the somebody did to him?"

I was pacing frantically and wringing my hands.

Deeka just gave me a solemn look.

"They locked him up in a crazy house!" I screeched.

"Geneva, calm dow—"

"Get out!" I screamed and walked into my bedroom, slamming the door behind me.

The following morning found me standing on the scale, the flat carousel of numbers spinning rapidly beneath the glass and then shifting indecisively back and forth beneath the needle until finally coming to a stop, dead center on 225.

I'd lost three more pounds!

Happy, I stepped off the scale and walked naked into the kitchen, where my bottle of Biothin pills was waiting on the table. I opened the top, plucked out two pills, and dropped them into my mouth.

An hour later I was strolling into the diner, my head held high, imagining that my weight loss was visible to everybody.

"Good morning!" I sang out as I rounded the counter and moved into the kitchen.

Arthur, the cook, looked up at me and laughed. "You're in a good mood, Geneva—what, you eat a cow over the weekend or something?"

His comment stopped me dead in my tracks. Arthur and I had had a love-hate relationship for years. We were both overweight, although he was grossly obese and couldn't take more than two steps at a time without wheezing. In fact, he'd grown so big over the past year that he was now using a cane to get around.

But I had to give it to him—he knew how to burn some pots!

Arthur had owned a restaurant in Harlem for a number of years, called Vesey's. But when Bill Clinton moved into the neighborhood and the rents tripled, he had to leave the space he'd operated from for more than twenty years.

Starbucks replaced him, and now he had to walk by it every day, jostling his way around yuppies and buppies carrying five-dollar cups of coffee.

Progress.

He joked about his weight all the time. Me, I never joined in on that humor. But he knew that I loved to eat, and every now and again he would make comments like the one that just sailed out of his mouth.

"Drop dead," I sang as I rushed past him and into the storage space that doubled as the employee locker room.

He just stomped all over my good mood, I thought as I tied my apron around my waist. "I'll show his fat ass," I said aloud as I dug into my pocketbook and pulled out my pills.

Noah

· · · · · · · · · · ·

I could hear the music a block away. I thought it was strange that someone was having such a loud party on a block filled with senior citizens.

The closer I got to my house, the louder the music became until finally I was just three houses away and figured out that the music was coming from my new neighbors' front window.

What the fuck?

I slowed when I got in front of their house; I half expected the front yard to be filled with people clutching forties and tightly rolled joints.

But instead I found two young men sitting on the front steps. Both were dressed in long white T-shirts and colorful pajama bottoms. Their heads were tied tight with red do-rags, and they laughed loudly as they passed a blunt between them.

My eyes rolled from them and up to the open parlor window,

where two large speakers thumped out Sylvester's version of "You Are My Friend."

This can't be happening, I thought to myself as I averted my eyes and climbed the steps to my front door.

The music seemed louder inside my house than it did on the street. I walked in circles for a minute, trying to figure out what to do. I moved to the kitchen, picked up the phone, and started to dial 911, but just as the operator answered I chickened out and hung up.

It would be obvious to them that I was the one who called. I'm sure they saw the look of disapproval on my face. I didn't want any trouble from those people—and they looked like they loved trouble.

Okay then, I would have to take care of it myself. Approach them like the mature adult I am and ask, very nicely of course, if they wouldn't mind turning down the volume—just a pinch.

Yeah, that's what I'll do.

I headed back out the front door and down the steps.

"Hey," I said, pushing their gate open and stepping into their territory, "I'm Noah Bodison, your neighbor," I said, extending my hand.

The two men looked at me, my hand, and then each other, but said nothing.

I slowly lowered my arm back down to my side. "I was wondering if you could turn down the volume some. It's pretty late and I have to get up early in the morning."

The two men continued to stare, as if I were speaking a foreign language. After a while, one of them smirked and then turned to the other and picked up the conversation again.

"Um, 'scuse me," I said, raising my voice. "Can you please turn the music down?"

I felt my patience slipping away, and I didn't care that the two men were twice my height and weight and could easily snap me like a twig.

They looked at me again, and the one who currently had possession of the blunt sucked on the tip and exhaled, sending a plume of smoke in my direction. "A'ight," he mumbled.

"Well, thank you," I said, and started back toward my house. Once inside, I waited for the music's decibel level to decrease, but after ten minutes, it remained the same.

"Fucking motherfucking fucks!" I screeched into the air.

This is just my luck, I thought as I climbed the stairs to my bedroom. I finally get rid of Chevy and now the entire cast of *Meet the Browns* is living next door.

Crystal

· · · · · · · · · · · · · ·

this is just great, I thought as I sat on the toilet, peering down into my underwear. My period had come and on a Monday morning. This was not the way I wanted to start my week.

I slid off the soiled Victoria's Secrets, stood, and stepped into the shower. I allowed myself to become lost beneath the powerful pulsating jets I'd had installed a year earlier. It had been a pricey investment, but my life had become so dismal that very often my morning shower was the best part of my day.

After I got dressed, I popped two Midols and headed out the door.

The day was starting off wonderful, and even though the weatherman had called for rain, there wasn't a cloud in the sky, which annoyed me to no end because I'd worn a raincoat and had lugged my long black umbrella.

When I got to the Eighty-sixth Street station, the platform was packed with wall-to-wall people, which told me that the MTA was acting the fool again. Finding a small space, I turned the volume up on my iPod and allowed Kirk Franklin to wash over me.

"Good morning, Ms. Atkins," Sheria, my new assistant, greeted me brightly.

I threw an unenthusiastic "Morning" at her as I started toward my office.

Sheria jumped up from behind her desk and followed me. Her hands were full of papers as she briefed me on the meetings and conference calls I had scheduled for the day.

"And oh, those came for you early this morning," she said as she pointed across the room at the flower arrangement that sat on the glass table by the window.

I moved toward them, and the closer I got, the lovelier they became. It was a beautiful arrangement of tropical flowers.

"Oh, Neville," I sighed as I reached for the card. Maybe this Monday my shower wouldn't be the highlight of my day.

"Can I get you a cup of coffee, Ms. Atkins?" Sheria asked as she placed the pile of memos and faxes on my desk.

"Yes, please. Decaf, a little cream, no sugar," I said in a faraway voice as I settled myself into my chair and lifted the small flap of the envelope that came attached to the arrangement.

"Will do, Ms. Atkins. And don't forget, your first conference call is in ten minutes."

I nodded as I pulled the card from the envelope and began to read.

Crystal,

I love you with all my heart. You are the one and only woman for me.

Love,

Kendrick

Before I even knew what I was doing, I'd flung the card across the room as if it were laced with some deadly substance.

I looked over at the flowers. Why was he doing this to me?

I stood and wrapped my arms around myself. My stomach was tied into knots; there were goose bumps on my arms. I began to pace.

Walking over to the window, I peered down at the people on the sidewalk.

Was he down there, watching and waiting?

My head began to ache.

Hadn't I made myself clear the other night? Could his persistence be considered stalking? Maybe I should call the police, report him. This behavior had to be in violation of his probation.

Okay, girl, pull yourself together, I told myself. You're becoming paranoid. It was one unannounced visit and now flowers.

That's how it starts, doesn't it? a small voice echoed in my head.

"Miss Atkins?"

I spun around.

"My God," Sheria said, walking toward me. "Are you okay? You're as white as a sheet!"

. . .

Somehow I made it through the day. Three conference calls, two meetings, and a luncheon at Sapa, a ritzy Vietnamese restaurant on Twenty-fourth Street.

I'd been distracted all day, and it showed.

A number of times during the meetings when I was asked a question I had to have the person to repeat him- or herself because my mind was on my problem and not on the tasks at hand.

I was jumpy too. I half expected Kendrick to come storming into the conference room, and at one point at Sapa, I thought he was one of the waiters.

By six o'clock I knew I had become completely unfurled, because when my phone rang I nearly jumped right out of my chair.

Sheria was gone for the day, so it was on me to answer the phone.

I watched the red light blink on and off as the phone continued to ring. I knew on the fifth ring it would automatically go into voice mail.

And that's just what it did, but then the next extension lit up and started ringing.

This went on for a good ten minutes, until finally I thought that I was going to lose my mind. Grabbing my purse, I bolted out of my office.

I loitered in the lobby for a while until I was sure Kendrick Greene wasn't lurking outside on the sidewalk. When I did gather up enough nerve to step outside, I headed straight for the curb and threw my hand up to hail a cab.

This could get expensive, I thought as I shelled out the eighteen-dollar fare to the driver. "Do you see a black Cabriolet parked anywhere?" I asked as I peered nervously out the window.

"What? Do I look like a detective to you or something?" he snarled at me.

Climbing out of the taxi, I looked left then right before sprinting to the entrance of my building.

"Ms. Atkins, welcome home," the doorman greeted me.

"Has anyone come by looking for me?" I whispered.

"No, I don't believe so," he whispered back, obviously amused by my strange behavior, "but I just came on at four."

"The cameras are still working in the elevators and in the hallways, right?" I asked, wringing my hands.

"Y-yes, I believe so . . . Are you okay?"

"I'm good. I'm good," I said, and walked to the bank of elevators.

A long, hot shower and a cup of tea later, I felt a bit calmer. Just as I was getting ready to put on some smooth jazz, the phone rang.

Looking at the Caller ID, I saw that it was Geneva.

"Hey, girl."

"I got fired today."

Geneva didn't sound upset.

"What . . . Why?"

"I attacked a customer," she said flatly, and I could hear her pulling on a cigarette.

"You did what?"

"He called me a cunt."

"Geneva, I—"

"I'll get unemployment, though, so whatever . . ."

"Whatever"?

"You sound really calm about it. You know, if you need some money—"

"I'm fine. I just wanted you to know," she said, and before I could say another word, I heard a soft click followed by a dial tone.

I stared at the phone for a minute. Geneva was certainly acting bizarre. I started to call her back but then changed my mind. I had my own problems to deal with.

Chevy

．．．．．．．．．．．

if I could smell myself, I'm sure that the ten other passengers in the elevator could smell me too. It's amazing what happens to your body after not bathing for seventy-two hours.

I jumped off the elevator. The long hallway that led to the double glass doors used to be covered in white carpet. A geisha-like woman would greet you just as you stepped off the elevator and take your shoes.

That was no longer. The white carpet had been replaced with an industrial-strength blood red, and who knew what had happened to the geisha girl. I guess that's what happens when a privately owned company goes public.

"Good," I whispered to myself as I pushed through the glass doors, "I beat the receptionist here."

I peeked down the long corridor. All was quiet, but I still tiptoed my way toward my office. I had to be as careful as possible—one of those overenthusiastic brown-nosing employees trying to make points with Anja could be lurking behind any one of those closed office doors.

I reached my office, slowly opened the door, and ducked in.

Whew!

Hurrying into the bathroom, I turned on the shower full blast. Just as the bathroom was starting to fill up with steam, I caught sight of myself in the wall-length mirror and almost fell over in shock.

My skin coloring was two shades darker than usual.

Raising my hand to my face, I pressed my index finger against my cheek and slowly allowed it to travel down to my jaw line. A clean line appeared. I was covered in grime.

Jumping into the shower, I scrubbed myself almost raw, and when I was done in there, I leaned over the granite sink and brushed my teeth until my gums began to bleed.

My weave was dripping wet. I didn't have a blow dryer, so I dried it best I could with the large and thirsty towels Anja had had brought in special from Thailand.

It wouldn't be a problem, really; I'd had my hairdresser sew in the wet-and-wavy synthetic hair—a change from the bone straight I'd been sporting all winter.

I lotioned my skin with Kiehl's body cream, sprayed my neck and wrists with Marc Jacobs's newest fragrance, and then wrapped the moss-colored towel tightly around me and walked into my office.

"What the fuck!" I yelped.

LaTangie was hovering over my desk, her hand resting on the papers in my inbox.

"Oh, I thought I heard the shower running. I was just going to check to see if . . . um, the pipes had broken."

What kind of lie was that? This girl was dealing with the master; she had a lot to learn.

I just glared at her.

She gave me an innocent smile before her eyes crawled over me. "Wild weekend, huh?"

"Get out," I ordered, walking toward the door and pulling it open.

LaTangie didn't say a word; she just batted her long lashes at me and sashayed through the doorway. Me, I slammed the door shut so hard, the vibrations could be felt out on the sidewalk.

I'd been trying to get down to Accounting for hours, but Anja was in Mexico, shooting me e-mail after e-mail concerning her Memorial Day extravaganza.

By two o'clock, I'd taken care of most of her requests and so headed down to the twenty-eighth floor, where Human Resources and Accounting were located.

"Chevanese," Myra Goldberg, a walleyed, frizzy-haired multiracial sister greeted me, "how are you?"

"Fine." I was curt; I just wanted to get to the business at hand.

"Now, on the phone you said you wanted to get an advance on your paycheck, right?"

I nodded my head and focused my vision over Myra's shoulder and on the potted ficus. I hated looking dead-on at Myra. The first time I'd ever met her, it freaked me out, because I wasn't sure if she was talking to me or the empty space beside me. I kept looking to my right and then found myself moving to my right in an attempt to put myself directly in her line of vision. Apparently I was; it just didn't seem that way to me.

"Yes."

"How much are you hoping for?"

"Hoping"?

"Seven hundred dollars."

My take-home after tax and health insurance was usually about $1,081.00. I hadn't opted to contribute to the retirement plan. Shit, I needed all my money now. Who said I would live long enough to retire!

"Hmm." Myra sounded thoughtful as she pecked away at the keyboard before her. "Give me your social, please."

I called it out and ticked off in my mind the New York City hotels that Anja had a good relationship with. They were all luxury properties. I could probably finagle a room for about fifty dollars a night. Maybe I'd even stay for a week or two. I'd show Noah, throwing me out, putting his hands on me like I was some bi—

"Well, it seems, Chevanese, that you've got quite a few creditors garnishing your paycheck, including Uncle Sam," Myra advised in a tight voice. I could tell right then that she was not fond of people who could not handle their finances.

" 'Scuse me?" I said, leaning forward.

"The. Federal. Government." Myra's tone was clipped, and when she leaned back in her leather chair, for a moment I swear her eyes lined up perfectly.

"Not only them, but"—Myra leaned forward again, her index finger poised over the Enter button on the keyboard—"American Express"

Enter

"Citibank Visa"

Enter

"Lord and Taylor"

Enter

"Saks Fifth Avenue"

Enter

"And of course your Melu-Melu membership."

My mouth went dry. They were all garnishing my check at the same time?

"That can't be right," I said in a weak voice. "There's a law . . ." I racked my brains to remember. "Only two garnishments at a time or something . . ." I faded off.

The room began to swim and I felt like I was going to faint.

Myra leaned back in her chair again and folded her hands across her pudgy stomach.

"That used to be the rule, but it changed right along with the bankruptcy laws last year."

Yes, yes, I was going to faint.

"How much," I squeaked. "How much can I get?"

Myra's right eye moved slowly to the screen. "Well, in total, your garnishments add up to nine hundred twenty-four dollars and twenty-five cents, leaving you with a take-home pay of one-fifty-six seventy-five."

I passed out cold.

Noah

....

I **don't know** how long the music went on like that, but I finally took two Tylenol PMs, stuffed some cotton into my ears, pulled the pillow over my head, and eventually fell off to sleep.

I woke up at ten and went into the bathroom for my morning piss. Still groggy, I made my way back to my bedroom, pulling the cotton from my ears as I went. Outside my window someone had started bouncing a basketball.

Snatching open the shutters, I peered down onto the sidewalk and saw that it was one of the young men from last night. He was now dressed in a blue and white Sean Jean sweat suit. The red do-rag was gone, and I could see clearly the gleaming cornrows that covered his head.

I watched as he bounced the ball between his legs, spun around effortlessly, and shot into an imaginary hoop. On the street sat a white Bronco. The windows were rolled up, the interior cloudy with smoke.

Why was this boy in front of my house bouncing his ball? He lived right next door—what was wrong with bouncing it in front of his house?

I closed the shutters and went to take a shower.

By the time I'd bathed and dressed, the ball bouncing had stopped and the Bronco was gone. The block was peaceful and I sent a quiet praise of thanks up to the Lord as I cracked two eggs and watched the yolk drop down into the frying pan.

After my breakfast cooked, I turned on WBLS and listened to Steve Harvey act the fool as I buttered my toast. My thoughts sailed to Will and what he'd said about Merriwether needing to see me.

This thing with my new neighbors had almost made me forget about that. Now as I picked up a slice of bacon and bit into it, the conversation floated back to me.

I don't know what Merriwether thinks she and I have to talk about, I thought as my eyes fell on my cell phone, which rested before me on the kitchen table.

I was curious as to what she wanted to tell me. Maybe I would call her, but not today . . . but soon.

Steve Harvey made a joke at his cohost Jackie's expense, and Nephew Tommy broke down with laughter. I laughed along until I heard screaming outside my window.

It sounded as if someone was being murdered! I leapt from the table and flew to the front door. Not thinking about my life, I snatched the door open and stepped out.

No one was being murdered. Well, not in the homicidal way. What was happening, though—in front of my house—was what looked like a double Dutch tournament.

There were six girls, ranging in age from about ten to eighteen. From what I could make out from the screaming that was going on, the fat girl with Afro puffs had had her jump already and was refusing to take her turn at turning the rope.

The one with the long blond braids, who couldn't have been more than eight years old, was swinging her index finger in Afro Puffs's face and inviting her to kiss her "black ass."

This was insane. Weren't these kids supposed to be in school?

Three of the six girls had hoisted themselves up and onto the fence, using it as a bench.

I was seething when I started down the steps.

The fence was as old as the house—over one hundred years— and I was sure that the weight of their fat Big Mac–eating behinds would send it toppling over.

"Excuse me," I bellowed.

All eyes turned to me.

"First off, do you mind? This fence is not for sitting."

The three girls sucked their teeth and slowly changed their position from sitting to leaning.

"It's not for leaning either," I said.

Rolling their eyes and cussing softly, they went to lean on one of the parked cars.

"You all are from that house, right?" I said, flinging my arm to indicate the house next door.

The girls didn't respond. Must be a family trait.

"Then why aren't you playing in front of your house?"

No one said anything, but after a few cut eyes and hisses, they moved the few feet to the front of their house and the game started up again.

Satisfied, I went back inside.

I would have to talk to the mother. I'm not going to live like this, I thought as I removed my plate from the table.

Just as I was preparing to wash the dish, the thumping sound of the basketball started up again, this time mixed with the heavy bass of a Ludacris cut, combined with the sound of children playing.

I stormed to the window and saw that the tournament had moved back in front of my house and the NBA wannabe had returned, as well as the Bronco.

The Bronco's doors were wide open, and the young men inside puffed on their joints and delighted in watching the ripe behinds of the young girls roll, bounce, and shake with every turn of the rope.

I watched on in disgusted awe until the sound of the telephone ringing broke my trance.

"Hello?"

"Hello, Noah."

"Zahn?"

"Yes, how are you?"

"I-I'm fine, and you?" We were being so formal with each other. I hated that.

"I'm fine." Zahn's response came in scratchy waves from New Delhi. He was still mad, I could tell from his tone. "And how are things in NYC?"

I didn't want the first conversation I had with Zahn since leaving England to be filled with complaints, but I so wanted to tell him about my neighbors from hell and how with every day that passed they seemed to be multiplying.

"Good, good."

"How are the girls?"

"They're fine."

There was a long silence. I knew Zahn wanted to know if I'd thought further about the adoption situation, and to tell the truth, I hadn't. In fact, in light of the million and one children living next door to me, I'd come to the conclusion that I hated children. Well, at least bad-ass ones.

"Have you thought any more about what we discussed?" Zahn finally asked.

I sighed heavily. I certainly didn't want to go down that road again. "Zahn," I said, my voice filled with irritation, "I just don't think that I am cut out to be anyone's parent."

I was being honest. What more did he want from me? If this would be the deciding point on whether or not we remained together, then so be it.

I loved that man's drawers and I would probably be a mental case for a year or so, but hey, I would get over it. Life goes on, don't it?

"Okay then, so I have to run." Zahn's tone was flat.

"Okay—yeah, I love—"

Click.

He was really angry and he was being unreasonable, not to mention selfish. My feelings weren't even being considered here.

I pressed End on the telephone and went upstairs.

The door to Chevy's room was open. Something was wrong with the knob, because I'd pulled that door shut I don't know how many times and it always popped right back open.

Walking inside the room, I looked around. Nothing had changed—it was still filled with Hefty bags full of Chevy's crap.

I shook my head. I don't know how she slept in there, I thought, as I stepped out and pulled the door shut again. Oh, that's right, I reminded myself as I headed toward my bedroom. She had been sleeping in my room.

For a quick second I wondered where Ms. Drama had gone off to. I hadn't heard a peep from her. She was probably traveling somewhere with her freak show of a boss, Anja.

I knew she'd turn up sooner or later. Chevy wasn't about to abandon the love of her life: her wardrobe.

I walked over to the window and looked down at the children on the sidewalk. They'd drawn a hopscotch board in chalk on the sidewalk right in front of my house.

The mother, whose name I'd found out was Cupcake, worked for the parks department. I'd spotted her leaving her house around six in the morning, dressed in her green parks department uniform, a cigarette dangling from the corner of her mouth.

The woman couldn't even leave the house quietly. It seemed as soon as she hit the sidewalk, she'd remember some task she forgot to tell one of her children, and instead of going back into the house she'd yell the child's name over and over again until he or she either came to the door or looked out the window, after which she'd recite the task and climb into her Hummer, rev the engine three or four times, and then screech away.

She must be off today, because there she was, puffing on a cigarette, sitting on her stoop, plaiting the hair of a young girl wedged between her fat thighs.

I looked up. The sky was a brilliant blue; it was a glorious day.

Moving from the window, I made up my mind that I would not spend the day dwelling on all the madness in my life but would get out and enjoy the sun.

Geneva

· · · · · · · · · · · · · · · ·

my hands were shaking—that's how I spilled the cup of coffee all over that customer.

It was an accident, and I was apologizing and trying to wipe at his suit jacket with a napkin when he said, "Get away from me, you stupid cunt!"

And before I knew it, I'd coldcocked him. It was a natural reaction.

I couldn't believe what I'd done. I was usually so cool and calm. I didn't normally allow the customers and their bad manners to get to me. But he called me a cunt, and them was fighting words.

I tried to help him up from the floor, but he skirted away from me. The flesh around his eye was already turning purple.

"Mister, I'm so sorry—let me help you," I said, reaching for him, but he had his cell phone out and screamed, "Get away from me! I'm calling the cops, you fucking crazy-ass cunt!"

There was that word again.

I rushed him, throwing myself on top of him and pinning him to the floor. I slapped him twice across his face and asked, "Do you kiss your children with that filthy mouth?" and then I snatched his cell phone from his hand and threw it across the room.

Some of the other customers ran out of the diner. Others looked around in shock, while still others hurriedly pushed 911 into their cell phones.

I was mad insane and almost knocked Darlene's block off when she grabbed me from behind.

"Hey, hey, it's me, Geneva," Darlene wailed as she ducked my swing. She wouldn't come near me again. Arthur was the one who finally dragged me off the startled man.

By the time the cops arrived, I was somewhat calm. I couldn't say the same for my customer, who was on the floor crying like a baby, folded into the fetal position and three different shades of pink.

Who was the cunt now?

After the officers had taken my story and the stories of the customers—and most hadn't seen the altercation from the start—they asked the victim, Mr. Chambers, if he wanted to press charges.

I held my breath and waited for his response. To tell the truth, I didn't even realize that my hands were balled into fists, but Mr. Chambers saw, and maybe the idea of another beatdown is what made him reply, "No, I don't want to press charges."

Chevy

· · · · · · · · · · · ·

I came to just as Myra was about to call the paramedics. My eyes fluttered open and locked onto Myra's hovering face.

There were a few people in the background, talking quietly among themselves.

"Are you okay?"

"Yes, I think so," I said as Myra helped me struggle to my feet. The other coworkers asked how I was feeling. Someone offered me bottled water and another offered me an oatmeal cookie.

"Do you have low blood sugar?"

"No."

"Are you pregnant?"

"Hello, no," I bellowed as I straightened my clothes. Smoothing my palm over my hair, I said, "I just missed lunch."

Myra gave me an incredulous look. The other people slowly moved out of the office and back to their cubicles.

"So would you like me to cut you a check?" Myra asked, picking up where we left off.

"Yes."

I took that check right to Chase and cashed it. When I returned to my office, I got down to the task of finding a place to stay.

"Yes, normally we would be able to comp a room for a La Fleur employee, but we're booked solid. The Cancer Society convention is in town this week," the woman at the Pierre Hotel told me.

I called ten hotels and got the same response.

Where the hell was I going to sleep tonight? I couldn't bear the thought of riding the subways, and staying at the YMCA was just as unappealing.

By the time seven o'clock rolled around, I was still seated behind my desk, trying to figure out what I was going to do.

At nine o'clock, when the cleaning lady came through, I had already decided. I would stay right there in my office. Shit, I had a large, comfortable couch. Who would know?

I forced myself to make small talk with the cleaning lady, and as soon as she left I locked the door to my office and stretched myself out onto the sofa for a good night's sleep.

I'd think about my fucked-up predicament in the morning.

That Friday, as I sat perusing my e-mails, LaTangie walked into my office without even a knock on my door.

"Don't you have any manners? It's polite to knock before you enter, you know," I said as I glared at her from behind my desk.

"I did, but you didn't hear it," she said, and tossed an interoffice memo onto my desk. Without another word, she turned and walked away.

That LaTangie was really getting on my last nerve. Not that I was in the best of moods to begin with. You try sleeping on a couch for four days straight. My neck was stiff, my back sore, and to make things worse, I only had three changes of clothes. I don't think anybody noticed I'd been rocking the same pieces on alternate days because I'd been spending most of my time in my office, behind my desk.

I'm sure the cleaning lady knew what was going down, because last night I forgot to take my panties off the handle on the sliding glass door. I only had two pairs of underwear and I had to wash the used one out at night. It wasn't like I was going to the Laundromat—in fact, there wasn't a Laundromat anywhere near Rockefeller Center as far as I knew.

She pretended like she didn't see them, but I knew she had.

I picked up the memo and began to read:

THE BUILDING WILL BE CLOSED FOR THE LONG WEEKEND.
A&B EXTERMINATORS WILL BE FUMIGATING FROM
MIDNIGHT TONIGHT UNTIL MONDAY AFTERNOON.
ENJOY THE HOLIDAY WEEKEND.

I read the words over and over again. The building was going to be closed all weekend? Where the hell would I sleep now?

I thought about the sixty dollars I had left from my paycheck. This would have to last me for the entire weekend.

Maybe it was time to break down and call Noah.

I reached for the telephone.

Crystal

· · · · · · · · · · · · · · · ·

the week had gone by really quickly, and for that I was grateful. I hadn't seen hide nor hair of Kendrick and I hadn't heard from him either. I began to feel like my normal self again. Maybe he had gotten the message and decided not to bother me anymore.

Noah, Geneva, and I were meeting at the Blue Water Grill for dinner and cocktails. The forecast had promised a high of 78 degrees, which would make the day feel more like summer than spring.

When I arrived at the restaurant, Noah was already there. He'd taken a table outside, which was fine with me.

"Hey, girl," Noah sang out as I approached.

"Hey yourself, good-looking," I said as he stood to embrace me.

"What's that you're drinking?" I asked as I settled myself into the wrought-iron chair.

"Gin and tonic."

My eyebrows rose. Noah was mostly a wine man. He'd usually only drink hard liquor when he was out clubbing, so this was unusual.

"I have had a hard week, Miss Girl." Noah laughed before he lifted the glass to his lips.

We'd spoken briefly about his problem. "The neighbors?" I questioned as I unfolded my napkin and dropped it into my lap.

"I like to refer to them as 'the devils.' "

"Haven't you spoken to the mother about all this?"

Noah smirked. "She's part of the problem, Crystal. She's just as loud and uncouth as the children."

"I guess the apple don't fall too far from the tree, huh?"

"You know that's right."

"I can't believe nobody on the block is complaining."

"I think they're afraid. You know, most of the people on my block are senior citizens. They're half blind and deaf to begin with. And besides, them kids are only playing in front of my house."

I shook my head in disbelief. "Do you think they singled you out?"

"I don't know, girl, but it certainly seems that way," Noah said, and caught the passing waiter by his elbow. "Another, please." Then he turned back to me. "So enough about me, what's going on with you?"

"Oh, nothing. Just the same old routine."

"You still running?"

"No, I'm just too tired. Why do you ask?"

"Well, Miss Girl," he began, and cocked his head to one side, allowing his eyes to fall down to my hips, "you are spreading something awful."

I knew I was. I'd been eating like a hog and not doing a lick of exercise. It was a struggle just to get in the dress I was wearing.

"It's water weight. I'm on my period," I said blandly.

"Is that the new term for old-age spread?" Noah jeered.

"Oh, shut up," I barked, and snatched my menu up from the table. "Have you heard from Chevy?"

"Not a peep—you?"

"Nope. But then, I haven't called her, and you know the only time Chevy calls me is—"

"When she wants money," Noah and I said in unison, and then broke down laughing.

"What's so funny?"

We looked up to find Geneva looming over us.

Geneva

....

think they were talking about me.

They claimed they were laughing about Chevy, but I didn't believe them.

"You look good, Geneva," Crystal said. "The more I see you with that new hairstyle, the more I like it."

"Yeah, I feel the same way," Noah concurred.

"Thanks," I said from behind my menu.

"So how's things?" Noah asked.

I put my menu down and looked at Crystal. I knew she told him—she told Noah everything. They wanted to play games, fine; I would play their stupid game.

"Oh, didn't Crystal tell you?" I said, my eyes boring into Crystal.

"Tell me what?"

Noah was so good at playing stupid.

"That I got fired," I said, pulling my box of Newports from my bag.

"Fired?"

Noah's eyes swung from me to Crystal. He did look surprised, but he had always been a great actor.

"For what?"

I lit my cigarette and inhaled deeply. "I attacked a customer," I said calmly as I blew a plume of smoke over his head.

The surprise on Noah's face seemed to spread, and then he smiled a bit and asked, "You're kidding, right?"

"Nope," Crystal said.

"Well, you don't seem to be worried about it," he said, picking up his drink. "I guess your man and your son will take care of you now, huh?" Noah laughed and threw his hand up for me to give him some dap.

I ignored the gesture. "I don't need no man to take care of me. I'll find another job."

"I'm sure you will, Miss Thang, I'm sure you will," Noah said before taking a large gulp of his drink.

There was a long, uncomfortable silence before Noah said, "You know, I really like Deeka—"

Before he could finish his sentence Crystal chimed in—and a little too eagerly, I might add—that she liked him too.

I hadn't forgotten about what I'd seen in the courtyard the day of the party. I had my eye on her, on both of them.

"Yeah, he's okay, I guess," I said.

What was I doing here? I didn't want to be here with them, these people who were pretending to be my friends. If they were real friends, why hadn't they said anything about my weight loss?

They were jealous, that's why. Jealous that in a few weeks I would be thinner than both of them!

"Geneva? Geneva?" Crystal's voice pulled me from my musings.

"What!" I snapped. Crystal, Noah, and the waiter were all staring at me.

"I'm sorry," I mumbled. "I didn't mean to snap at you."

"Okay, baby." Noah was using his calming voice. He reached up and patted my hand. "The waiter just wanted to know if you were ready to order."

After I put my order in I asked Crystal if I could use her phone. I needed to remind my mother to give Charlie her antibiotics on time; she was suffering with an ear infection.

When I was done, I set the phone down near my plate. Halfway through dessert, it began to ring. I picked it up, and as I passed it over to her, I caught sight of the number that was calling.

It was Deeka's.

Noah

....

i **didn't know** what the hell was going on with Geneva, but she was creeping me out. It was like she was on some bipolar roller coaster. One minute she'd be laughing and joking, and the next she was brooding or just being plain old nasty.

When she mentioned that she'd lost some weight, I looked closely at her and did see that her face looked smaller.

I wanted to know which weight-loss program she'd jumped on this time, and she almost took my head off with her response: "I ain't on no goddamn weight program. I'm just eating right and exercising."

Well, that was news, because Geneva ordered a medium-rare steak, mashed potatoes, and french fries!

Crystal and I had just exchanged glances, but we didn't dare say a word.

"That's nice," I said instead, and turned my attention to my salmon.

When the waiter came around asking if we were interested in dessert, Crystal and I both leaned back in our chairs, patted our stomachs, and shook our heads no. But not Miss Geneva—oh no, honey child—Miss Geneva ordered apple pie à la mode and inhaled it before we could even blink.

Eating right and exercising, my ass!

Crystal asked if she'd heard from Chevy, and in between bites of her pie and ice cream Geneva said she had—in fact, they'd spent some time together the other week, even took in a Broadway show.

I didn't believe what I'd just heard, and from the look on Crystal's face neither did she.

"What show?" Crystal asked.

"Drama, We All Got It," Geneva announced proudly.

Now I had to laugh—loud, hard, and long.

"What's so funny, Noah?"

"I-I just want to know how much you had to pay her to go see that show."

Geneva threw her fork down onto the dessert plate. "I didn't have to pay her anything. She wanted to go."

"Chevy wanted to go see that? It just doesn't sound like her cup of tea," Crystal said.

"Well, Chevy has changed," Geneva said, retrieving her fork again.

"Has she?" I said, wiping the tears from the corners of my eyes. "Well, I'd like to meet this new Chevy."

Geneva was about to say something when Crystal's cell phone began to ring. Geneva picked it up and as she passed it to Crystal, something in her eyes changed.

At the time, I didn't know who was on the other end of that call, but it certainly had Crystal all jumpy. Well, that and the fact that Geneva was eyeballing her.

Crystal ended that call quickly, but I could tell it had unnerved her because her lip was twitching.

After that, no one said anything for a while and Geneva looked like she wanted to kill Crystal.

Both Crystal and I flinched when Geneva reached for her purse. I know it's crazy, but I half expected her to pull out a gun, but instead it was her wallet. She threw some money down onto the table and mumbled something about having to get home to Charlie.

She left without even saying goodbye.

Crystal

· · · · · · · · · · · · · ·

between the wine and the good weather, I was flying. I was on cloud nine!

Noah and I had had three more drinks after Geneva stormed off like a maniac. It was just my luck that Deeka had chosen to call me at that moment to find out if I'd come up with a place for him to propose.

I was sure that if Geneva saw that it was his number she would have said something. But she didn't, so Noah and I just chalked it up to this new erratic behavior of hers.

I told Noah of Deeka's intention to ask Geneva to marry him, and he laughed and said, "Hmm, he better take Miss Thang to get her head examined first!"

Sure, Geneva was behaving like a freak, but maybe she was premenopausal too. I certainly felt that I was.

Women have been known to act a little nutty when going through The Change.

I wanted to tell him about Kendrick but decided against it. I was afraid that if I mentioned Kendrick, I might talk him up.

I floated down the sidewalk toward home. My head was light and I didn't feel as if I had a worry in the world, until I turned the corner and walked right smack into Kendrick Greene!

"Hey, hey," he said, catching me by my elbow and steadying me.

Grinning stupidly, I looked up into his face, and for a moment I didn't even know who he was. When the realization hit, terror took over.

Snatching away from him, I stumbled backward and began digging feverishly into my purse for my cell phone. "I'll call the police!" I shrieked.

Kendrick calmly watched me. He was wounded; I could tell by the look in his eyes.

"Crystal, do you honestly think I'm here to hurt you?"

His voice was soft. I stopped digging and concentrated on his face. Were those tears sparkling in his eyes?

"I—I," I stammered, suddenly feeling foolish.

"I don't know what to say to you," he started, not making an attempt to come closer to me. "I apologized a million times in my letters. Do you want me to write it in the sky? Because I will."

I could feel myself melting.

"Everyone deserves a second chance—you're the one who told me that, and now here I am asking for one and you're refusing to give it to me."

I felt ashamed.

"Can we get a cup of coffee and talk? I have a lot to tell you," he said, holding his hand out to me.

I just stared at it.

"Please," he said, his tone pleading.

Everything in me screamed: *Don't do it!*

But the heart is stubborn and wanting, and I found myself placing my hand into his.

Chevy

. . . .

I called Noah twice and both times I got the answering machine. Called the cell phone and it went straight to voice mail. I slammed the phone down without leaving a message.

That faggot was ignoring me. I guess he was still mad.

I racked my brain as to what I was going to do. In any case, I needed to get some of my clothes from his house. He couldn't deny me that—it was my property, after all.

The clock on my computer screen told me that it was 6:15. Most people had left around noon, but I was going to try to stay here for as long as possible.

At seven o'clock, I heard the exterminators marching through the corridors and I knew my time had run out. I pulled a plastic Saks Fifth Avenue shopping bag from my bottom drawer, grabbed a pair of Red Monkey jeans and a T-shirt from the closet, my one pair of clean underwear, a tube of toothpaste, and my toothbrush, and headed out the door.

Once I got outside, my head would clear and a solution would come to me, I was sure of it.

By ten o'clock I still hadn't decided what I was going to do. I tried to call Noah again, but the message that came on after I dialed the number informed me that Cingular had cut me off due to lack of payment. I could, however, dial 911 in case of an emergency.

I strutted along, head held high. I wanted to cry, but I wouldn't. I couldn't!

I am a grown-ass woman and will handle my situation as such, I thought.

I roamed the streets until I found myself in Alphabet City. The streets buzzed with activity. Salsa music blared from open windows and oversize SUVs.

My stomach grumbled loudly when I passed a Coochie Frito restaurant that advertised STEW CHICKEN, RICE & BEANS W/SIDE SALAD—$7.50

What the hell, right?

I hadn't realized I was devouring my food at such an alarming rate until I looked up and saw the woman who'd served me staring.

"More?" she called out to me in her heavy Dominican accent.

Yes, I wanted more, but with the two Cokes my meal had totaled a full ten dollars, leaving me with fifty dollars until next payday, which was a week away, and I still didn't know where I was going to sleep.

"No, thank you," I said, and gathered my belongings.

After walking for another hour, I stumbled across an apartment building that had a blue and yellow neon sign that blinked HOURLY RATES.

I was so damn tired; I just needed to lie down for a while. I walked past the place twice before I finally made up my mind to go in.

The lobby was fitted with one lone sofa that looked so battered and infected, I wouldn't allow my worst enemy to sit on it. A number of scantily clad women stood around babbling to each other in Spanish. There were two men, one dressed in a black shirt that was unbuttoned down to his navel, exposing his hairy chest, and another who looked like a reject from *Miami Vice*. Both wore dark shades, but I could feel their eyes probing me as I walked in.

"How much?" I asked the hefty, pimply-faced man behind the glass enclosure.

"How many times you want?"

"How many times?"

"Yeah, yeah, how many times you want . . . *uno, dos, tres* . . . how many times?"

I stared at him for a moment, trying to decipher what it was he was trying to relay to me, and then it clicked, "Oh, how many hours!"

"*Sí,* " he said, pointing to the cardboard sign that hung on the wall behind him. On it, scrawled in black marker, were the hourly rates:

One hour = $15.00
Two hours = $25.00
Three hours = $35.00
Four hours = $45.00
Five hours or more = $50.00

I thought about the fifty dollars I had left. I couldn't waste all my money on sleeping—I would have to eat.

"Two hours," I said.

The room was as small as a walk-in closet and smelled of cigarettes and pussy. The bathroom was outside in the hallway and was shared by the four other rooms on the floor.

I peeked in and saw that the toilet was antiquated and filled with brown water.

The sink, maybe white years ago, was yellow and flecked with black mold. I didn't even want to move that shower curtain and look at the tub.

The bed was twin-size, and I braced myself as I pulled the blanket back. The sheet looked clean. I touched it—it was wrinkled and rough-feeling.

I looked around for critters and found none. After moving the only other piece of furniture up to the door—a chair—I debated for a few moments whether to turn off the lights or not, but I had to; I couldn't sleep in a lit room.

I hit the switch and the room went dark except for a tiny stream of light that was coming off the wall.

"What the hell," I said as I moved to inspect it. "Well, I'll be," I mumbled. A hole had been bored through the wall, directly into the next room. I pressed my eye against the hole and could clearly see a man stretched out on his back in the bed.

He was huge, his belly round and soft. Naked except for the brown socks he wore, he was grinning, the heels of his feet knocking happily together.

"Come on, baby, come to Daddy," he squealed to someone I had yet to see.

A few seconds later, a woman stepped into view. I could see her only from her rib cage down.

"Have you been a bad boy?" the woman asked.

"Yes, yes, I have—very bad!" the man screeched, and the heel knocking increased in speed.

"Shall I punish you, then?" the woman asked, and she slapped something against the palm of her hand. The sound was sudden and I jumped.

The fat man began to squirm, and that's when I noticed his hands were tied to the headboard.

"Okay, then, you know what happens to boys who misbehave, don't you?"

Thwack!

I jumped again.

"Yes, yes, I do!" the man shrieked, and began thrusting his pelvis into the air. "Please punish me, *pleeeeeeeeeeaaaaaaaaaaaseee!*"

Thwack!

This time the woman didn't slap her hand with the object but brought it down hard across his thigh.

The man jumped and his head rolled on his neck in ecstasy.

Thwack!

Thwack!

Thwack!

The weapon struck every part of his body, leaving his skin welted and red—and still he called for more.

When the woman had had enough of torturing him, she took a few steps forward and roughly parted his legs with her knees.

I waited for another strike, but when she brought the object down again it just made a soft thudding sound on his stomach, and it was then that I saw it was a dildo. Long, pink, wide, and bulging with artificial veins.

It looked like a sex toy made for an elephant!

"Are you sorry yet?" she purred.

The man shook his head no.

"Are you sure?"

Me, I looked at the size of that thing and wanted to scream, "He's sorry, he's sorry!"

He nodded his head yes, and the woman began to slowly drag the rubber dick across his stomach and then down between his legs. His penis, which was small by my standards, stood as straight as a pole, jerking slightly whenever the dildo touched it.

One of her hands disappeared from sight and was followed by a sucking sound, which seemed to increase the man's excitement; his head began to buck on the pillow.

When her hand returned to view, her middle finger and forefinger were glistening with saliva, and then she promptly slid them up his anus.

In and out, in and out—until the man began to whimper with joy.

After a while she removed her fingers, grabbed hold of the dildo, and lined it up with the entrance to his anus.

My heart clenched up and I bit down on my lip.

With one quick move, she shoved it into him. The man screamed, but he didn't beg her to pull it out.

She pushed and pushed until more than half of it had disappeared up inside of him.

I thought I was going to be sick, but I couldn't stop watching.

She used both hands to work the dildo, pumping it as if she were handling a plunger instead of a fake penis.

When he finally shot his load, the woman was glistening with perspiration.

She walked out of view for a minute, leaving the dildo lodged in the man's behind. When she returned, she had a washcloth in her hand, which she used to wrap around the toy before giving it a hard tug.

A wet, squishy sound accompanied its dislodgement.

The man made a soft noise in his throat and then released the loudest fart I'd ever heard!

Afterward, as the man dressed, they exchanged small talk as if they'd just had coffee and not engaged in a sick sexual act.

Before he left, he counted off ten $100 bills, patted her on the ass, and said, "See you next week, Tangie."

Noah

· · · · · · · · · · · ·

after the theatrics at Blue Water Grill, it was good to get some fresh air.

The night was balmy, such a complete opposite of London evenings.

I'd had four gin and tonics, and it showed. I was weaving down the sidewalk and chuckling at my drunkenness.

When I turned the corner and stumbled upon an empty Coke can, I kicked it with the toe of my shoe and watched as it sailed through the air and landed in the street. "Goal!" I screamed, thrusting my arms up into the air.

I didn't care who saw me. I was feeling real good.

Three houses away, I saw blue light emanating from the parlor floor of my neighbors' home. It looked like they had the television right up against the window. Stupid asses, I thought to myself.

As I moved closer, I saw that the television wasn't just close to the window—it was in the window!

Not only that, they had dragged their sofa out into the front yard. I couldn't believe my eyes.

Propped up on the sofa were Cupcake and four of her children. Two of the older boys were tending the hibachi grill in the corner of the yard. I sniffed and the distinct smell of barbecued chicken filled my nose.

What the fuck?

They had a whole backyard to grill in and a nice-size living room to watch television in. Why in the world would they choose to do all this in their front yard?

I moved closer to the parked cars, hoping to scurry by them unnoticed, but just as my hand touched my gate, Cupcake turned around and hollered, "Hey, neighbor!"

I forced a smile and lifted my chin in greeting. In return, Cupcake saluted me with the forty she was holding.

Jeez!

I let myself into my home. Closing and securing the door behind me, I started up the stairs to my bedroom. Although I could clearly hear the reruns of *Sex and the City* outside my window, I was thankful that it wasn't the thudding gangster rap that I'd had to endure earlier in the week. I could deal with Kim Cattrall any day.

When I hit the top landing, an alarm went off inside me. The light was on. I didn't remember leaving that on.

The door to the extra room was open.

Okay, that wasn't unusual—like I said before, that door pops open all the time.

I looked down the hall and saw that the door leading to the roof was slung back on its hinges.

Now, I know I didn't do that.

And just like that, I knew I'd been robbed!

Chevy

· · · · · · · · · · · ·

needless to say, the twenty-five dollars I'd paid to sleep was spent watching the live freak show.

So there I was again, riding the train, and as tired as I was, I couldn't go to sleep. I just kept hearing LaTangie's name ringing in my ears.

There couldn't be two people in this city with that same name. It had to have been her. I couldn't wait for Tuesday, when I could expose her prostituting ass to Anja.

It was Saturday morning, and I'd decided that enough was enough and jumped off the train at Eighty-sixth Street and walked straight to Crystal's building.

I knew I looked a hot wreck, but I held my head high, walked right up to the doorman, and said, "Crystal Atkins, please."

The doorman recoiled and made a face that told me my breath was foul.

"And you are?"

He knew who the hell I was. How many times had I been to visit Crystal?

"Chevy Cambridge."

He looked me over and then picked up the black telephone. "Ms. Atkins, a Chevy Cambridge is here to see you," he said, and then listened for her response, his eyes never leaving me.

"Yes, I'll send her right up."

He'd hardly finished speaking before I was headed to the elevator.

Crystal was standing in her doorway when I stepped into the hallway. She pulled her blue silk robe tighter around her when I approached.

"Hey, girl," she said, "everything okay?"

I put my best face on. "Of course. I just haven't seen you for a while and I was in the neighborhood and thought I'd drop in."

"At seven-thirty in the morning?"

"Crystal, girl, I was at this party a few blocks away," I started my lie as I stepped past her and into the apartment.

Crystal closed the door and followed me into the kitchen. "I'm starving. What you got to eat?" I already had my face in the refrigerator.

"Chevy, you smell . . . funny."

Ignoring her comment, I reached for a plastic container. "What's this?" I asked, shaking it in her face.

Crystal's eyes moved from me to the container and back. "Um, eggplant lasagna, I think."

"Is it fresh?" I asked, peeling off the lid and peering inside.

"Two days old . . . but Chevy, what's going on? I—"

"Okay, okay," I moaned, pulling the door open to the microwave and pushing the dish inside. "I got a little wild and ended up in this alley with this guy, and you know . . ." I said, shrugging and grinning mischievously.

"No, I don't know," Crystal said, pulling out a chair and sitting down.

It did sound ridiculous, me screwing some man in a back alley. Geneva, yes, Noah, yes—Chevy, no fucking way!

"Well, I don't know what you want me to tell you." I avoided her probing eyes as I pulled the container from the microwave.

Crystal silently watched me wolf down my meal. When I was done, she lowered the boom.

"Noah said he put you out."

My head snapped up. "He didn't put me out. I left."

Crystal smirked at me.

"I did!" My voice was climbing. "You always believe everything Noah says. You all treat him like he's Christ."

Crystal raised her hands in surrender. "I didn't say I didn't believe you, Chevy."

"Yeah, well, anyway," I mumbled, looking around the kitchen. When I turned my attention back to Crystal, she was sneaking a glance at the wall clock above the sink.

"Am I keeping you from something?" My tone was snide.

"Well, um, yeah—I have to go to the office today."

"On a Saturday?"

"Yeah, I'm trying to catch up."

Damn, I was hoping I could take a shower and a nap, maybe even spend a night or two.

"Oh," I began in a sweet voice, "I really wanted to spend some time with you."

Crystal's face bloomed with surprise. "Oh, really?"

"How about this," I said as I fitted the lid back onto the empty container. "I'll just hang out here until you get back, and then maybe we can grab a movie or dinner."

"No!" Crystal yelped as she shot right out of her seat. "I— the apartment is going to be fumigated, and so you can't stay . . . won't be safe, with the fumes and all."

What the hell is going on with this fumigation shit? Was every building in New York City infested with vermin?

"Yeah, I know," I said as I slowly rose from my chair, "maybe next time."

"We can still hook up later on if you want."

"Yeah, I'll call you."

I wanted so much to ask her for a couple of dollars, but I didn't. I just picked up my shopping bag and started toward the door.

"What's in that bag?"

"Oh, um, just an outfit I have to return."

Crystal

· · · · · · · · · · · · · ·

I closed the door and watched from the peephole until Chevy stepped onto the elevator. After double-checking the locks, I went to my bedroom.

"Is she gone?" Kendrick queried from the bed. He was propped up against two pillows, the white sheet draped loosely across his naked body.

"Yes," I said, and climbed in beside him.

He wrapped his arm around me and planted a gentle kiss on my forehead. It felt good, being there next to him, but it didn't feel totally right.

How he ended up in my bed is simple:

I was drunk, he was there.

I was lonely, he was there.

I was horny, he was hard.

We never did have coffee. We had every intention to, but after we took our seats at Merchants restaurant on Columbus Avenue, it just didn't seem right to be sipping coffee when all the other patrons were throwing back alcohol.

"How about a bottle of Cristal?" Kendrick had suggested after I'd spent five minutes perusing the cocktail menu.

"Are we celebrating?"

"Every breath is worth a celebration, don't you think?"

I nodded my head in agreement and then said, "Not Cristal, though. You heard about what the maker said about African Americans drinking his champagne, right?"

Kendrick nodded his head. "Then we'll have Moët."

A small smile tugged at the corners of my lips. He was still suave.

We spent more than two hours at the table talking about everything and anything, including his time behind bars for drug possession. He kept that part of the conversation light, but I saw the sadness in his eyes and my heart tugged in my chest.

"I'm a new man, Crystal, I swear I am," he said, reaching across the table and taking my hand in his. "Won't you let me show you the new me?"

We left Merchants hand in hand. It was just like old times.

When we reached the front of my building, he pulled me to him and said, "Aren't you going to invite me up?"

He was being presumptuous, and that was a bit of a turnoff for me, but then he leaned in and kissed me. It was a long, deep, probing kiss that made my knees weak. The pounding that began down between my legs was loud enough for the entire block to hear, and then I heard myself say, "Yes, of course."

We were like two schoolkids. He had me pressed up against the wall of the elevator, his hands moving slowly over my breasts, down between my legs, clawing at my thighs.

By the time I pushed the key into the lock of my door, my blouse was halfway off.

Breathlessly, we stumbled onto the couch, where we frantically undressed each other.

"You're just as beautiful as I remember," Kendrick said, standing back and admiring my naked body. His eyes went wet and I felt the tears spill down onto my breasts as he gently sucked my nipples.

I had his member in my hand; it was as hard as steel. I cried out in anticipation.

When he positioned himself to mount me I was damn near crazed, but a small, sane voice called out to me from the back of my mind, and I pressed my palm against his chest. "Condom, we have to use a condom," I whispered.

"What shall we do today, sweetheart?" Kendrick's voice pulled me from my reverie.

"I don't know, baby," I said, yawning. "We could spend the day in bed?"

Kendrick turned to me, his penis already hard and knocking against my thigh. "Sounds like a plan to me."

Noah

••••••••••

they'd gotten my laptop, my stereo, my iPod, and my entire collection of watches. After the police left I didn't sleep a wink, not that I could if I wanted to. I was too damn scared.

The officers casually mentioned that there had been a rash of burglaries in the neighborhood over the past month.

Wasn't that just as long as Cupcake and her tribe had been living here?

Of course, they were nowhere to be found when the police rolled up. Criminals have radar where the law is concerned. Two minutes before the cops arrived, their front yard emptied out and the house went dark and quiet.

Figures.

I couldn't wait for the sun to come up, and then I couldn't wait until nine o'clock.

After calling ADT and agreeing to pay the $100 rush charge for them to come the same day, I contacted Harold's Ironworks to come and install bars over all my windows—and then after all that, I called Crystal.

"Crystal, girl, they robbed me! Them no-good, lowlife motherfuckers jacked me like Bush jacked Iraq!" I wailed.

"Noah? Noah, what happened now? Who robbed you?"

I hushed my voice and moved into the living room. "Them project Negroes from next door."

"Your new neighbors?"

"Yes!"

"Are you sure, Noah, because—"

"Yes, I'm sure. Who else could have done it?" I snapped.

"Okay, just calm down. Take some deep breaths. You sound like you're about to hyperventilate."

I did feel a bit light-headed. I crumpled onto the couch. My heart was racing. "Can you come by?"

"To Brooklyn?" Crystal asked unbelievingly.

She was beginning to sound like Geneva. Geneva considered Brooklyn foreign territory; she claimed that in a minute one would need a passport just to get in here.

"Forget it. Shit," I mumbled.

"No, no, Noah, I didn't mean it like that. I—I'll be there as soon as I can, okay?"

"Okay," I whispered before pressing the End button on the telephone.

I made Crystal spend the night. Shit, she didn't get here until damn near four o'clock in the afternoon. "Where you been?" I screamed when I swung the door open.

I had a bat clutched in my hand and my butcher knife shoved into the waistband of the military fatigue pants I wore.

Grabbing her by the wrist, I quickly yanked her inside.

"Noah, what the hell?"

I closed the door and secured the three new locks I'd had installed that morning.

"Noah, you look like you're on speed or something." Crystal's voice was filled with concern.

"I ain't on no goddamn speed—I'm scared!" I shrieked, and went to peek out the front window. "Did you see them, huh, did you?"

"See who, Noah?" Crystal asked, moving up behind me. I swung around, raising the bat. "Don't be walking up on me, Crystal," I warned.

Crystal just glared at me before reaching for my wooden weapon.

I'd been holding on to that bat so tightly and for so long that it had become another appendage.

"Let. It. Go!" Crystal said between her teeth, and, finally, I did.

"You've got to calm down. You're acting like a crazy person," she said, setting the bat in the corner and then leading me to the sofa.

"There are just a few kids out there playing innocently."

"Oh, they're far from innocent!" I said before slumping down and allowing my head to fall dramatically back onto the cushy pillow.

"I-I can't stay here anymore. I have to move. I have to get out," I cried.

Crystal settled herself beside me, taking my hand in hers and giving it a comforting pat. "It'll be okay, Noah."

I looked into her face, and her eyes seemed far away. Now, why did that immediately make me feel like the "okay" she was talking about didn't have jack to do with me?

Chevy

• • • • • • • • • • • •

I started up the street, mumbling to myself. When I reached the corner, I saw something that was quickly becoming extinct in New York City. A pay phone. I rushed to it, my pride nothing but vapors now. Snatching the receiver off the cradle, I decided that I would call Crystal and tell her my whole sordid story, but my fingers had their own idea, and the number I found myself dialing belonged to a man I dated some time back, named Carl.

"Hey, this is Carl!" his effervescent voice answered. For a moment my words were locked in my throat. It took a minute for my mind to realize just who I'd called.

"C-Carl?"

"Yep, this is he. Who's this?"

I'd met Carl about a year ago as he was climbing into his late-model C-Class Mercedes and I was cutting out early from work. It was the car that caught my eye, not Carl, and when I turned to get a better look at the smooth curves of the machine, Carl was frozen, staring at me like I was the most beautiful creature he'd ever seen.

"Hey," I had ventured, already knowing that I would never spread my legs for him. He was short, wide, and balding. The bifocals he wore looked as if they were an inch thick, and his bottom lip was a plump pink piece of jutting meat.

"M-me?" he said unbelievingly as he used his index finger to indicate himself.

"You see anyone else around?"

Carl looked slowly over his shoulder and then back at me. "No."

I had him from hello.

In just under twenty minutes he revealed that he was the owner of the Sunshine Laundromat franchise.

He had twenty locations throughout Queens and Brooklyn. He wasn't married, had no children, and still lived at home with his mother in Hempstead, Long Island.

I almost felt bad for what I was about to do to that brother.

Three months and thousands of dollars in "loans" later, I cut it off.

Why?

Well, he started talking about marriage and children. Funny thing, though, he never pressured me for sex and I hadn't given him more than a kiss on his chubby cheek.

Although I did slip my hand down into his crotch from time to time—just to keep hope alive, if you know what I mean.

When I told him it was over, he cried like a baby. Or should I say like a bitch.

"Hey, Carl. It's me—um . . ."

"Chevy?"

Oh, God—it's been almost a year and this man still remembers my voice?

"Yes, it's Chevy."

"Oh my goodness. Chevy, Chevy . . . how are you?"

It was Christmas all over again for Carl. From the sound of his voice, I had made his fucking year!

"I'm—I'm, good. How about yourself?"

"Good, good," he squealed.

I could imagine him pacing the floor, giddy with excitement, his swollen belly quivering with joy. Ugh!

"I opened three more Laundromats," he continued.

"Oh, good for you . . . Listen, I need a favor."

"Anything!" His voice climbed another pitch.

"I'm in a bit of a pickle, and I need someplace to crash . . . just for the night."

For a minute I thought my magic had worn off, because for a long time he didn't say a word. But just when I was about to speak, his voice came back, calm and even.

"Where are you? I'll come and get you."

Crystal

· · · · · · · · · · · · ·

You're such a good friend," Kendrick had said after I hung up the phone with Noah. "A good woman," he added, and squeezed me tightly.

God, it felt good to be wrapped in his arms again. I breathed in his scent, twirled my fingers through the hairs on his chest— just plain ole relished in the moment!

"Why, thank you!" I laughed before tilting my head up and planting a kiss on his soft lips.

"Did I tell you how much I missed you?" Kendrick's brown eyes burned into me.

"A hundred times," I said, and planted another kiss on his lips.

"Did I tell you how much I love you?"

I smiled. "Two hundred times."

"Is that all?" He laughed, squeezing me tighter. "Damn, I'm behind."

I grinned; it was like old times again. Maybe this was the start of a new beginning for us. I hoped so.

We made love again. It wasn't feverish like the first two times; it was slow, sensual, gentle. We took time with each other, nibbling, kissing, licking, sucking . . .

When we were through, I was exhausted. All I wanted to do was remain in Kendrick's arms, but I'd promised Noah, and so after a catnap, we finally pulled ourselves from the bed and headed into the shower.

Geneva

....

When **I** left Crystal and Noah, I was fuming. I couldn't even wait until I got home to call Deeka and confront him. I knew that was his number on Crystal's cell phone. I just couldn't wait to hear the explanation he was going to give me, so I stopped at a pay phone and called him.

When he answered, I let him have it.

"Why the fuck are you calling Crystal?"

"What? Geneva, is that you?"

"Are you fucking her? Are you?"

"Of course not—what's wrong with you? Why would you say something like that?"

"Liar, liar, liar!" I screamed, and began banging the receiver against the black and silver box.

Who knew how long I'd been standing there screaming and

banging the phone, but when I finally came to my senses, all that was left of the receiver was a few bits of plastic and wire.

I turned around and saw that a crowd had gathered behind me.

Off in the distance, I could see a beat cop walking steadily in my direction.

I turned and hurried away.

When I got home, there were more than twenty messages on the machine from Deeka. And while I sat, smoked, and stewed, I listened as he left fifteen more. He even came by, calling up to me from the sidewalk, but all I did was chuck his clothes at him from my window.

I was done with him and that damn Crystal too!

Chevy

. . . .

how Carl made it all the way to Eightieth Street and
Columbus Avenue from Hempstead, in weekend travel traf-
fic, in less than an hour, I didn't know.

He was driving a Range Rover now, dark blue with a beige interior, tinted windows. The truck came to a screeching halt in
front of me.

When Carl opened the door, he was grinning. I tried my best
to offer him a pleasant smile, but I saw that his stomach had increased in size over the past year and the shirt he wore was barely
covering the swell, exposing the yellow stretch marks embedded
in his skin.

I swallowed back the bile rising in my throat and told myself
that this was no time to be particular.

"Hey, Carl, thanks so much," I said, ducking the hug he'd

jumped out to give me and running to the passenger side of the truck and jumping in.

Carl took his seat again, pulled the door shut, and glanced into the rearview mirror and then down at his two-sizes-too-small Polo shirt.

He tugged self-consciously at the ragged bottom and then announced in a quiet voice, "I was doing some housework when you called."

"That's okay, sweetheart," I said, reaching over and touching his knee. "I'm just glad to see you."

It took forever to get to Hempstead, and Carl had rambled on nonstop during the hour-and-a-half drive. I felt trapped in that Range Rover and wondered why this time he hadn't taken the same route that he'd streaked through to get to me.

"Do you want me to stop to pick up something to eat?" Carl asked, turning to me. He hadn't really looked at me the entire time we'd been in the vehicle, and when he finally did, his eyes didn't fall on my face, but lingered on my breasts for a while before moving down to my thighs and then up to my crotch.

I folded my hands over my lap.

"Sure," I said, and turned my gaze back to the road.

His mother was away in Florida; he'd bought her a condo in Miami.

"She spends most of her time there now," he said as he struggled to maneuver the key into the lock while holding the three bags of food from Kentucky Fried Chicken.

I'd never been to Carl's house. We always met at the high-end restaurants I chose from the Zagat's restaurant guide. And I sure as shit never let him know where I lived. I knew early on that Carl had stalker potential.

The house was dark and smelled musty.

"Turn on some lights," I said as I followed him through the living room and into the dining room.

The dining room table, a bleached white wood, was littered with newspapers and what looked like months and months of mail.

"Sorry," Carl announced, embarrassed. "I don't get a lot of visitors," he said as he swept the pile of papers to one side and set down the bags of food.

The dining room led directly into the dated kitchen. I took in the Formica counters and dark wood cabinets. There were dishes in the sink and the floor looked grimy and sticky.

"So, what, the maid quit?" I half joked.

Carl pushed his fists into his fat hips and laughed. "Yeah, something like that."

He hadn't bought anything to drink, so when I asked what he had around to wash these drumsticks and biscuits down with, he disappeared into the kitchen and returned with a tall glass of cherry Kool-Aid.

I hadn't had Kool-Aid since I was ten years old! I guess some folks still believed that Kool-Aid was something other than water, sugar, and coloring. What the hell, I thought, and before I knew it, I'd chugged down two glasses of the stuff.

"So what happened to you? Did you get evicted or something?"

I guess the question was bound to come up. I wiped the grease from my lips and licked at the red sugary corners of my mouth before leaning back in my chair and folding my arms across my chest. "Something like that," I said.

Carl's face was blank for a minute, and then a small smile began to spread across it, and before long he was laughing, open-
mouthed and uproariously.

I smiled stiffly; I could clearly see that Carl had five teeth
missing.

After we ate, he showed me to the guest bedroom; the walls
were paneled with dark wood. A twin bed sat in the middle of
the room atop a bland orange shag carpet.

I am allergic to cheap—and even more allergic to outdated—
always have been, and now I resisted the urge to scratch the itch
that had suddenly crawled beneath my skin.

I had to remind myself again that this was no time to turn my
nose up at anything less than five star. But it was hard, 'cause this
shit was just a step up from the roach motel I'd spent two hours
in last night.

"The bathroom is down the hall to your left," he said, hand-
ing me a pale yellow towel and matching washcloth.

"Thank you."

We stood there for a while. He didn't seem to know that I
wasn't about to undress in front of him. "Was there something
else?" I asked.

He was staring at the plastic bag I'd been carrying my belongings in.

"Do you need something, um, washed?" he asked, his eyes
never leaving the bag. He licked his lips. What was this lip licking thing? I assumed he'd been watching too many LL Cool J
music videos.

My eyes moved to the bag and then back to him. "No—well,
yes, but I'll handle that after I take a shower."

"I can do it for you if you like."

Was that perspiration dripping down the side of Carl's face?

Did dirty laundry turn him on? Maybe that's why he was in the Laundromat business!

Sick fuck.

"Thank you, but no thank you," I said sternly, and with that he turned and walked out.

After I showered, I rummaged through the medicine chest in search of some deodorant and lotion, but all I could find was an old jar of Tussie and some Vaseline. Damn, I felt like I was back in the seventies.

The towel wrapped tightly around me, I fell into the twin-size bed and promptly dropped off to sleep.

I don't know how long I'd been out when I was stirred by the sound of heavy breathing. I slowly opened my eyes and found that my towel had fallen open, exposing my nakedness.

Still groggy, I peered through the darkness and my eyes lit on Carl, who was standing over me, butt naked, stroking his dick!

"What the fuck are you doing!" I screeched, sitting up and grabbing at the bedspread. "Get out!"

Carl was in another world; his eyes were blank and teary. "Carl!" I screamed again as I tried to cover my nude body.

Carl chuckled seductively with each stroke, and I felt my stomach turn over.

"Carl?"

"All that time, all that money, all that love I wasted on you. I was just a play toy for you, wasn't I, Chevy?"

He still wasn't looking at me; he spoke into the darkness.

My heart began to gallop. I had to think fast.

"No, baby—you got me all wrong. You weren't my play toy. I really cared for you. It's just that—"

"Shut up!" he bellowed, and finally his gaze fell on me. "I am going to fuck you, do you understand me? I am going to fuck you because you owe me at least that," he said calmly as he let go of his dick and took a step toward me.

I looked wildly around for something to protect myself with, but there was nothing. Fear gripped me, but disgust still had the stronger hold. I peered down between Carl's legs and saw the knob of a penis gazing back at me.

Fuck!

"Look, look, we don't have to—" I started, but then quickly changed direction. "I have herpes!" I said, finally catching hold of the spread and pulling it over me.

"That's okay," Carl said wickedly. "I have condoms."

I was doomed, doomed!

"Lie back," he murmured as he unfolded his hand. In his palm he held a small square of plastic. The letters glowed green: GLOW-IN-THE-DARK PLEASURE, it read.

I was terrified, but I knew that my slight 130 pounds wouldn't even put a dent in Carl's 200-plus frame, so I did as I was told.

"You're going to enjoy this, bitch." He sneered.

I closed my eyes and prayed.

He ate me out first.

It was a painful experience, painful and loud. He chomped away like my twat was a piece of overcooked beef. He lapped at it, sucked, and gnawed until I thought I would pass out from the pain. When I couldn't take any more, I yelled down to him, "Hey, man, I'm a woman, not chicken bone. You won't find any gristle there!"

What came next, I'm embarrassed to say.

He climbed on top of me and shoved that knob of a dick into me, which wasn't far-reaching at all, but I wanted it over and done with, so I behaved like he'd just stuck twelve inches into me.

"Oh, Daddy, you're so big!" I moaned.

"I know, I know." He labored heavily as he banged into me like a jackhammer. My head had been too close to the headboard to begin with, and after three of Carl's massive thrusts, it was smashed against it. Five thrusts in and the top of my skull was sore. By thrust number ten, I had a migraine coming on.

"Shit, I'm coming, Daddy, I'm coming!" I squealed and found his nipples (which were bigger than mine), giving them a hard twist.

"*Yiiiiiiiiiiiiiiiiiiiiiiiiiiip* . . . yip . . . yip . . . yip . . ." he bellowed like a hyena.

If not for the fear, I would have burst into laughter.

He shuddered, slobbered something masquerading as a kiss on my mouth, and then collapsed on top of me.

"I-I can't breathe," I managed just as Carl began to snore.

Crystal

. . . .

I spent the night over at Noah's, but the entire time my mind was on Kendrick. I felt like a giddy schoolgirl, my stomach swimming with butterflies. I tossed and turned all night, which would have normally irritated Noah, but he was too wired to sleep and so was pacing in front of the three windows along the wall of his bedroom.

"You see, see!" he kept saying whenever something new began to occur outside the house. "Crystal, they're chirping!"

"What?"

"Chirping," he emphasized, and then held his hand to his mouth as if he held a walkie-talkie. "Chirping!" he repeated.

"What's that, Noah?" I asked sleepily. We'd argued about me sleeping in his bed. I wanted to sleep in the extra room, Chevy's old room, but he wouldn't have it.

"Chirping, with those Boost mobile phones," he explained

while his thumb jerked back and forth, pressing an imaginary lever.

"So?"

"So? So!" Noah squealed as he turned and faced me. "There are two of them and they're standing three feet apart, chirping to each other!"

I was still confused as to what chirping was but thought it best not to press Noah in his unstable state of mind.

"Oh, damn," I said, and rolled back over onto my side. I wished he would just shut up; I needed to be alone with my thoughts . . . with my memories of last night.

My stomach was doing backflips, and I could feel myself becoming moist. I hurriedly shoved my hands between my thighs. If I was careful, I might be able to give myself a little pleasure without Noah noticing.

"There are six of them now, Crystal!" Noah screeched, kicking the bench at the foot of the bed in anger.

I removed my hands. Guess not.

Chevy

. . . .

i **had to** fuck him twice. Twice! After the second time I knew I
wouldn't be able to stomach a third, so while he was sleeping I
eased out of the bed, dressed myself, snuck through the house in
search of money—change, really, so that I could get on the rail-
road—but what I found was the motherload!

What made me pick up that Bible that was lying on the desk
in the study? I don't know. Shoot, maybe it was Jesus himself.

I opened the Bible and it flipped right open to the spot where three
hundred dollars in crispy new twenty-dollar bills had been stashed.

I was out of that house and down the driveway in the blink of
an eye. I had no idea in which direction the Long Island Rail
Road lay, but I would walk all night if I had to in order to get
away from Carl Matherson and his doorknob dick.

I would walk straight to Manhattan . . . shit, clear to Tim-
buktu if need be!

Noah

. . . .

That damn Crystal.

I wanted her to stay another night. I practically begged her.

But she didn't. She couldn't, so she claimed, saying she had to get back home because she had exterminators coming to the house. That sounded like a lie to me.

When she left, she got the full monty with regard to what I had been complaining about. Cupcake and her crew had a grill made out of an oil drum in the front yard, and guess what they were roasting?

A hog!

Cupcake had the audacity to send one of her little nappy-headed heathens over to invite me to the cookout.

Can you believe that shit?

You would have thought we were having our annual block

party, because she'd blocked off the entrance to the street with her Hummer and before I knew it there were children playing in the street, and Guatemalan ice hacks selling their frozen treats, and only God knows where the clown came from.

But the pièce de résistance was the black cowboys, propped high on their steeds and offering rides to the kiddies, five dollars a pop!

"Hey, man, c'mon over. I got swine, baked sweet potatoes, potato salad, butter beans, corn bread, and Kool-Aid!" Cupcake screamed over the music at me when I returned from walking Crystal to the train station.

I just kept walking, pretending that I hadn't heard a word.

Surprisingly, the cookout wrapped up by eleven. I was prepared for one of their all-night soirées. So when it suddenly went quiet, I didn't know what to do with myself.

I'd developed a twitch, and at the sound of a child's voice, my eyelids would go spastic. Now I stood there tense, waiting for a sound, a noise, a thump, something—nothing happened, it remained quiet.

After some time and few glasses of wine, I was relaxed. I even put in Floetry's latest and let their European soul wash over me.

I was good and drunk when Merriwether crossed my mind, and so I reached for my cell phone and dialed her number.

"Yes, hello—may I speak with Ms. Merriwether Beacon?" I heard myself say in as sober a voice as I could muster.

"This is Merriwether." The response was dry.

"Oh, hey, Merriwether, this is Noah."

"Noah?"

"Noah Bodison," I said. "Your husband . . . I mean, ex-husband, gave me your number."

Silence.

I cleared my voice and continued. "He said you wanted to speak to me about something urgent."

"Noah, is that really you?" Her voice had softened, and for some reason I imagined her gray around the temples and wearing a hairnet.

A giggle escaped me and I muffled it with a fake cough. "Pardon me," I spouted.

"Noah—oh my God, it's been a long time."

I thought back. It had been a while. Exactly how long I wasn't sure, so I said, "It's been a minute—so what's up?" I hoped against hope that she didn't think I was still into pussy.

"Um, well, not a whole lot. I am single again, but I guess you know that since you saw Will."

"Yeah," I half said, half burped, and then looked accusingly over at the empty bottle of Pinot Grigio. " 'Scuse me," I said.

"Sure, no problem. Are you still living in Brooklyn?"

"Well, kind of. I spend most of my time in London—you know, where I saw you."

"Oh, yeah," she breathed, and I could hear some rustling in the background. "How's the family?"

Okay, this bitch just wasn't going to get to the point, was she? She didn't know my people—we'd had one sweaty, funky, sex-filled night and that was all!

"So what did you need to speak to me about?" I asked, getting straight to it.

I thought the connection had gone dead, because the silence was so long.

"Maybe we should meet?" she said.

Meet?

"I think that anything you need to say to me can be said over the phone, Merriwether."

"No, no, not this, Noah. I need to see you face-to-face."

Now I was getting worried.

Chevy

· · · · · · · · · · · ·

When I arrived at St. Patrick's Cathedral, it was just past six in the morning. Fifth Avenue was a ghost town, and I found myself standing on the stone steps with the priest.

"Good morning, sister," the bent black man greeted me.

"Yeah, morning," I grumbled. I'd spent most of the night walking the dark neighborhood roads in search of a Long Island Rail Road station. I felt like I was trapped in an *Outer Limits* episode. At some point I must have crossed into the white part of Hempstead, because all of a sudden I looked up and a police cruiser was on my heels.

"Are you lost, lady?" a white female with cropped bleached-blond hair and Bette Davis eyes asked me, after lowering the flashlight she'd damn near blinded me with.

I straightened my back, clutched my plastic bag closer to me, and said, "Yes, I am lost."

I didn't know how true those words were until I followed the aging monsignor into the church and settled myself down onto the wooden pew.

So this is what I've come to, I thought as I sat staring at the white world's likeness of the savior. His head was tilted forward, but his eyes seemed to watch me. I turned my gaze away.

The last time I'd been in church I must have been twelve years old. I had been raised a Catholic. My mother had switched from the Baptist faith to Catholicism when she married my father. My maternal grandmother, however, was a Bible-thumping Baptist, and the summers I spent with her found little me wedged on Sunday mornings between my grandmother's wide hips and the scrawny ones of my cousins, listening to the word passed down by the minister.

I always felt that the best part of the service was the choir. They would get to singing and I would somehow float into the aisle on the wave of the music, stomping my feet and clapping my hands, gripped by the Holy Spirit!

I laughed to myself. Those were good days—what had happened to those days?

My eyes found JC's again.

"We had a good relationship a long, long time ago," I said, on my feet now, walking toward him. "What happened?"

JC just watched me. I moved closer.

"Did you forsake me?"

"You forsake yourself."

I froze where I stood and my heart skipped three beats. Had JC actually spoken to me? To me, Chevanese Cambridge?

This was a miracle! I fell down to my knees and tried hard to remember the prayers of my youth, but for some reason all my mind was able to dig up was the tune and words to that rap song that was so popular a few years back: *"Everybody in the club getting tipsy!"*

I clasped my hands together and shook my head wildly. There had to be something good in my mind, in my heart, in my soul . . . I concentrated harder and then I heard: *"Jesus walks . . ."*

Kanye West's tribute to Christ.

I opened one eye and peered shamefully up at JC and muttered a pitiful "Sorry, that's all I can come up with."

"I'm sure it's okay," the voice said again. I hadn't taken my eyes off the statue. His lips hadn't moved. Perhaps JC was speaking to me with his mind.

"Thank you," I responded.

"No problem," the voice said, and I realized it was coming from behind me. I spun around on my knees.

"You!"

Crystal

· · · · · · · · · · · · · · · ·

Kendrick called and said he would meet me for brunch, but I told him that I had a doctor's appointment at ten and that he should meet me after that.

I'd set up this appointment weeks ago. Dr. Spade was one of the few doctors I knew that worked on Sunday, and that fit right into my schedule.

I sat on the table dressed in the green and white paper robe, my feet crossed and swinging while I waited for Dr. Spade to come in.

I was actually smiling, and that wasn't like me, especially at my once-a-year gyno visit. I hate the nakedness, the cold gel, and the even colder steel stirrups, but it was a necessity in this day and age, and so I felt it was better to grin and bear it than to have an attitude. And besides, I truly had something to be grinning about.

Kendrick Greene was back in my life. Well, I should say the new and improved Kendrick Greene.

We'd shared a lot in the two days we'd spent together. I hate to say it, but having him in my life made me feel like a whole woman again.

"Crystal, how are you?" As Dr. Spade walked in, his sky blue eyes danced.

"I'm fine." I smiled and moved myself into position. A dark-haired, dark-skinned nurse followed him into the room.

"Hello, I'm Sharon," she said, offering me a broad smile.

Dr. Spade sat behind the small steel desk, and peered down at my chart. "I see you're going to be forty next month, Crystal."

Don't remind me.

"Yep!"

"I'll give you a referral for a mammogram, okay?"

"Yep!"

"But you have been checking your breasts on your own, right?"

Of course I had, and lately they seemed to have grown a size.

"Sure have." While I didn't really feel the need to mention it, something in me said I should: "And they've been sensitive for nearly a month now."

Dr. Spade looked away from chart. "A month?"

"Yes."

He laid the chart down on the desk and asked me to drop the top of my gown.

I focused on an empty spot on the wall while he rolled my breasts in his hands. Normally, I allowed myself to think about mundane things, but today for some reason I imagined Dr. Spade's hands were Kendrick's ... not just Kendrick's but Neville's as well. Kendrick had the left breast and Neville had the right one and before you knew it my imagination was in full swing, because I could feel each of their mouths, hot and wet on my nipples.

"Crystal?" Dr. Spade called my name.

I snapped back to reality, ashamed of my fantasy.

"Everything seems fine," he said.

"Oh, good," I said, pulling my gown back up over my breasts.

"So is there anything else?"

"Yeah, um, I want to get some birth control pills," I said shyly.

Well, if this thing with Kendrick and me was real, we would just naturally want to drift back to the days when we could enjoy each other without the hindrance of condoms.

Dr. Spade smiled. "No problem, but we have to give you a pregnancy test before we prescribe anything."

"Of course."

Geneva

. . . .

by Sunday morning I was so tired of the sound of my ringing phone that I ripped it from the wall.

By noon, my son, Eric, was coming through the door.

"Ma!" he called out to me. I was in my bedroom, playing Candy Land with Charlie.

I walked into the living room. "Yes?" I responded calmly.

Eric walked toward me, looking everything like his father. "What's going on with you? Deeka's been blowing up my phone like a madman."

I shrugged and went to sit on the couch. "Nothing," I mumbled.

Eric came to sit beside me. He watched me for a minute, his face swirling with concern. "You don't look well. Are you okay?"

What the hell did he mean, I didn't look well? I looked fabulous. Why, just this morning I was admiring myself in the mirror and my reflection said, "*Guuuuurrrrl*, you look good!"

"I'm fine," I said, touching my face.

Eric sighed, leaned back into the cushions of the couch, and asked, "So what's up with you and Deeka?"

Who the hell was he? I was the adult here, the parent; he had no right asking me about my personal business. Did I ask him about what was going on with him and the girl he was shacking up with? Hell to the no, I sure didn't!

"Mind your goddamn business," I snapped, and jumped up off of the couch.

Eric's face twisted with surprise and then hurt.

"Ma, why are you speaking to me like that?" he asked, reaching his hand out to me.

Why *was* I speaking to him like that? This wasn't like me, snapping at my baby for no good reason.

"I-I'm sorry, sweetie," I moaned, melting back down to the couch again. "Mama's just been a little stressed out, with losing my job and all."

Eric took my hand in his. "You know you don't have to worry about money, Ma. I got you until you can get back on your feet again. Deeka got us gigs rolling in left and right, and——"

I snatched my hand from his. "I don't need your goddamn charity!"

It was Eric's turn to stand. His eyes were wet. "Okay, then," he mumbled, and shoved his hands deep into the front pockets of his jeans. "I'll just go say hello to Charlie, and then I'm out."

"Whatever," I said, and turned my face away from his penetrating stare.

Noah

. . . .

merriwether was kind enough to come to Brooklyn and meet me. I guess she sensed my hesitation in leaving the borough.

We would meet at Bread Stuy, the neighborhood coffee shop located on Lewis Avenue off MacDonough.

I was halfway through my second cup of coffee and slice of red velvet cake when she finally walked in, thirty minutes late.

I almost didn't recognize her. When I last saw her, she was petite and shapely, with long flowing tresses. What was standing before me now was a woman who was barely five-four and weighing a good 190.

She'd cut her hair off and was now sporting short bleached-blond locks. Her nose was pierced and the blood red lipstick she wore took away from her golden complexion.

"Noah?"

I looked up into the brown eyes of a stranger. "Yes?" I said, my mouth crammed with cake.

"Merriwether Beacon!" she shrieked, and threw her fat arms out at her side.

I stared blankly at her.

"Merriwether," she said again, slowly lowering her arms and looking a bit miffed.

"Of course," I said, suddenly springing to life.

Damn, I thought, what a few years could do to a person. "You look fabulous," I lied as I stood and gave her a halfhearted hug.

"Thank you, so do you," she said, and took the seat across the table from me. "So how have you been?"

I sighed. Hadn't we covered this over the phone the other night? I glanced at my watch. I didn't want to stay long—Cupcake and her crew were probably having a meeting to decide how they would violate my house a second time.

"Fine—so what did you want to talk about?"

Merriwether looked over her shoulder and through the pane-glass window. I followed her gaze. No one was out there, just a line of parked cars.

"Well?" I pressed.

"You see," she began, looking down at her hands. She seemed nervous and unsure of how to break whatever news she had.

God, I hoped that she wasn't going to tell me she had a disease or something. I thought back. Yes, we'd used a condom, but nothing was a hundred percent, was it?

I shook the worry off me; I'd had at least three AIDS tests since I'd been with her and they'd all come back negative.

"When we were together, something happened . . . I mean, I found out something not too long after, and . . ."

She stopped midsentence, wringing her hands and looking around at the would-be writers that filled the coffee shop, all tapping away on their laptops, sure they were producing the next *New York Times* bestseller.

"Yes?" I urged.

"Well, it's like this," she said, and then took a deep breath. I leaned in close and waited.

Crystal

· · · · · · · · · · · · ·

"It can't be," I said.

"Well, these tests are pretty reliable, but we can give you a blood test just to make sure," Dr. Spade said.

I had been in shock before, or at least I thought I had, but as I sat there in the backless office chair, I felt like the world as I knew it had just dropped away. I figured this is what people mean when they say they feel as if the rug has been pulled out from beneath them.

"But I just finished my period," I lamented, looking desperately at Dr. Spade for some type of explanation.

Dr. Spade folded his hands and gave me a penetrating, thoughtful look. "It's not uncommon for women to continue getting their periods while they're pregnant. The bleeding is not truly a menstrual period but rather early pregnancy bleeding."

I felt like someone had just punched me in my gut. How could this have happened? I was careful. I always used a condom!

"But how?" I sputtered, already feeling the tears well up in my eyes.

"Well, you say that you used protection, but Crystal, you know that nothing is one hundred percent effective." Dr. Spade leaned back into his chair before adding, "Nothing except abstinence."

Noah

• • • • • • • • • •

i know that!" I screamed. "I know that nothing is one hundred percent effective!"

I was more than upset and jumped up from my chair, sending it tumbling over.

All of the would-be writers closed their laptops and watched me with wary eyes.

"So what are you saying?"

Merriwether still hadn't gotten down to the nitty-gritty of things, and we'd been sitting there for more than half an hour.

"Say it!" I bellowed.

By then Lloyd, one half of the husband-and-wife owners, had come from behind the counter and was standing behind me, urging me to calm down. He placed his hands on my shoulders and I roughly shrugged them off.

He was taller than I was and probably outweighed me by 150

pounds, but I didn't care—I had enough adrenaline pumping through me to beat his ass, as well as every man and woman in that place.

"Tell me!"

Merriwether swallowed hard, snatched a glance over her shoulder again, turned wet eyes on me, and said, "We have a daughter."

Crystal

• • • • • • • • • • • •

cradled my stomach all the way home. I cradled my
stomach and laughed and cried in between the disbelief. I was
pregnant. Two months gone. Due in January.

My God.

I walked dreamily past the doorman and didn't even remember pressing my floor on the lit elevator panel. When the ringing
sound of the phone finally brought me back to reality, it was one
o'clock and I had been sitting on my sofa for more than an hour.

"Crystal, I'm down here at the doctor's office. What are you
doing home?" Kendrick's panicked voice came at me.

I had forgotten all about Kendrick coming to meet me. My
thoughts were wrapped up in receiving blankets, baby booties,
and Pampers.

"Huh?" I said.

"I was out there waiting for over an hour. When you didn't

answer your cell phone I went into the building. Do you know that there are twenty-four gynecologists in that building?"

I didn't know that. Why would I know that?

"Yours was number sixteen." He laughed, but I could detect the annoyance in his voice.

"Oh" was all I could muster.

"Are you okay, baby?"

Suddenly Kendrick calling me baby didn't seem as soothing as it had over the last three days.

In fact, it felt dirty. I was carrying another man's child. "Baby" was not the appropriate name for me . . . at least not coming from Kendrick.

"I'm not feeling very well. Can I call you tomorrow?"

The silence was long and heavy.

"Sure, sure . . ." Kendrick's voice quaked a bit. "Can I bring you something?"

"No," I said, and abruptly hung up the phone.

Noah

· · · · · · · · · · ·

daughter?"

"Yes," Merriwether whispered.

"We?"

"Yes, us." Merriwether emphasized that fact by moving her hand between us as if fanning a flame.

"No, no, that can't be," I said, shaking my head furiously left and right. "I am a gay man!" I screamed. The patrons chuckled, and I'm sure I heard someone say, "Like that means something these days. I guess he's the only one who hasn't heard of the down low syndrome."

Merriwether's eyes moved warily around the café before settling on me again. "Do you really want to discuss this here?"

I didn't want to discuss this at all. Obviously she was lying, but why?

"What do you want?" I said, thrusting my fists into my hips and leaning forward a bit. "Money, is that what you want?"

Merriwether's face went from embarrassment to confusion before finally settling on anger.

"Money? Do you think I been searching for your good-for-nothing low-down faggot ass for money?"

Someone in the background yelled, "Tell him, sister—we been independent for a long time . . . got our own goddamn money!"

I just glared at her. "Then what, then, because when I slept with you . . . a long, long, long time ago, I might add," I said, making sure my eyes made contact with all of the faces that watched me, "I was confused." I punctuated that with a head roll and a snap of my fingers. "But not too confused not to use a condom."

It was Merriwether's turn to roll her eyes and snap her fingers. "And that condom—broke!"

My mouth fell open and then clamped shut again. I pressed my index finger to my chin and thought back. Had it broken? I truly couldn't remember.

"You were fucking me so hard, you didn't even notice," Merriwether added with a smug look.

Now I felt like an idiot. "Maybe we shouldn't discuss this here," I said, moving toward the door.

"Oh, no, let's," she said, blocking my exit.

Crystal

· · · · · · · · · · · · · ·

i walked into my bedroom and then back into the living room and then into the kitchen, and opened the refrigerator and then closed it again.

I did that at least ten times, or more, I can't remember. All I knew was that I was pregnant. I was pregnant and I supposed I should be happy, and some part of me was, but there was a small part that wasn't.

Well, it was obvious the child I was carrying belonged to Neville.

Neville, a lifelong bachelor and playboy. Not just a playboy, but a gigolo! He slept with women for profit . . . for money!

Could I have a baby by a male prostitute?

I walked back into my bedroom and went to stand at my window. I could clearly see the inside of Central Park, littered with people, but especially women and their children. There were baby carriages everywhere.

Would I be one of those women in seven months?

I placed my hands on my stomach again.

Wasn't a baby something I'd always wanted?

Yes, it was, but not this way. I never wanted to be a single mother. I wanted to be married. I wanted the house, the husband, and the white picket fence.

This is not at all the way I planned it. Not even close.

The tears began to spill then, and I didn't know if I was crying from joy or sadness . . . I think it was a little bit of both.

Chevy

....

Yeah, it's me. Who did you think it was, God?" The bum who had harassed me on the train just the other day was now seated in a pew, peeling a tangerine.

I rose to my feet and brushed at my pants. I felt like an idiot. Here I was, thinking that JC was actually speaking to me . . . I was so embarrassed!

"Looks like you're homeless to me," he said, and reached down and pulled my bag up from the floor. "Or behind on your dry cleaning," he said with a laugh.

I took a step toward him. "Those are my things—give them to me!"

"No problem," he said, and tossed the bag at me.

After peeling off two slices of the fruit and shoving them into his mouth, he dragged the back of his filthy hand across his lips, burped, and said, "So how's things?"

"Fuck you," I spat, and stormed down the aisle toward the doors.

"Hey, hey," he called after me. "This is a place of worship. Have some respect!"

"Fuck you!" I bellowed again.

"God speaks to and through all of us," he yelled. "Even the homeless, lost, and displaced!"

I slammed out of the church and hit the sidewalk running.

Geneva

· · · · · · · · · · · · · ·

I had just dialed the first three digits of Crystal's telephone number when Eric walked in. I was going to tell her off and then advise them which one of my body parts she and Deeka could kiss before damning them to hell.

"What are you doing back here?" I asked, and then my mouth fell open. Deeka was right behind him.

I slammed the phone down and picked the sugar bowl up from the table. Without a word, I flung it across the room. It barely missed Eric and shattered against the wall just centimeters from Deeka's right ear.

"What the hell, Geneva!" Deeka screamed, rushing toward me.

"Get out!" I hollered. "Both of you, get out!"

I really don't know what happened after that. The events are still blurry, but I do know that both Deeka and Eric tackled me, throwing me down to the ground.

Charlie was screaming, "Don't hurt my mommy!" in the background, and I was calling my man and my son every cuss word in the book!

When it was all said and done and I was somewhat calm, Deeka had a long scratch on his forehead and Eric had a busted lip.

Noah

· · · · · · · · · · ·

"I have my . . . *our* daughter out in the car, waiting to meet you," Merriwether said.

I couldn't move, but about five or six patrons jumped up and rushed the large pane windows.

"W-what?" I said, astonished. "She's here . . . outside, here?"

"Out in the car."

I looked over her shoulder. There were a number of cars parked on the street. My eyes slowly scanned each one of them. And finally fell on a dark blue Honda Civic, where I saw an older woman sitting in the backseat, smiling down at something . . . at someone.

Merriwether was smiling too, her hand extended to me. "C'mon. She's beautiful."

I walked as if in a dream, my hand tightly clasped in Merriwether's. The owners of Bread Stuy, Lloyd and his wife, Hillary, urged the patrons to give us some privacy, gently grabbing people by their elbows and pulling them back inside the coffee shop.

My heart was beating a million miles a minute by the time my feet hit the sidewalk, and I could feel the perspiration streaming down my armpits and sides and pooling on the waistband of my jeans.

"Mama, roll down the window," Merriwether said, making a winding motion with her hand.

The older woman looked just like Merriwether, except her hair was a lustrous silver color.

"Well, hello, Noah," she sang, her rosy cheeks glowing. "I've been waiting a long time to meet you." She extended her hand.

I think I nodded my head; my body from the neck down was numb. I wanted to smile, but my mouth wouldn't stop twitching.

"This is Destiny," Merriwether said as she yanked me closer to the car.

This wasn't happening, it wasn't happening. I was dreaming—yeah, that was it. I was dreaming and . . .

My eyes lit on four curly pigtails wound with pink ribbons.

I closed my eyes.

Wake up, wake up! I screamed in my head. This is a dream!

"Open your eyes, Noah," Merriwether demanded, and gave my hand a painful squeeze.

And I did, and found myself looking down into the smiling face of an angel.

"Hi," the angel said to me, "my name is Destiny. What's yours?"

Crystal

....

I'd picked up the phone to call Neville a number of times, but each time I chickened out and hung up.

I'd spent the entire night twisting and turning, grappling with the turn my life had suddenly taken. My appetite was gone, but I forced myself to eat some oatmeal. It was only right; I couldn't very well starve my child, now could I?

My child? God, that sounded so strange, but so right!

A smile tickled the corners of my mouth, and something warm wrapped itself around me. Suddenly I was filled with happiness; the worry lying heavily on me just a minute ago had magically disappeared.

This was my life, I was a grown woman, and I needed to start behaving accordingly. I was going to have this baby, no matter what Neville said. I didn't need him to raise this child. I had me, my mother, family, and friends . . . all the love anyone could ever hope for.

I reached for the phone; I would call Neville, make the announcement, and advise him of my intentions.

Just as I my hand touched the slim black shell of the phone, it rang, startling me into a fit of giggles. "H-hello," I answered, trying hard to hide my laughter.

"Crystal!" Noah screamed.

Oh, good. Neville should be the first one to know, but Noah would most likely be the constant father figure in this baby's life, so why not share the good news with him first?

"Hey, Noah, I've got great news—"

"I've got great news!" Noah screamed back.

"Well, your news can't be better than mine," I said, falling back onto the down pillows on my bed.

"I bet you it can!" Noah's voice was spilling with excitement. I assumed that Cupcake and her family must have moved out.

"Well, let me tell you mine first," I said.

"No, no, me first—you're not going to believe this!"

"No, Noah, let me tell you my news first. My news is totally unbelievable!"

I took a deep breath and then spouted, "I'm pregnant!"

And at the same time Noah shouted, "I have a daughter!"

We both went silent and then said, "What?"

"I said, I'm pregnant, Noah." I was sitting up now. Surely I'd heard Noah wrong. "What did you say?"

"I said, I have a daughter. I'm a father, Crystal!"

Noah

. . . .

When that little girl looked up at me and spoke, I saw in her face generations of Bodisons—men and women.

She looked so much like me, it was as if Merriwether had had nothing at all to do with her.

Destiny looked like I had carried and birthed her myself!

I gotta tell you, I went weak in the knees. I'd only just met her, but I was already head over heels in love with her.

"My word, she looks just like you," the grandmother said.

"Tell me something I don't know," I muttered as I reached for the door handle. I had to have her in my arms.

She was short-limbed like me, and we had the same fair skin and curly hair. (Of course, my curls were chemically induced, but still . . .)

"Hello, Destiny," I said as I lifted her from the seat. "I'm Noah. I'm your father."

Just saying those words brought on a shower of tears.

"You got a boo-boo?" Destiny asked, touching my tear-streaked cheek with her stubby fingers.

"No, no," I blubbered, pressing her close to me. "I got you and that makes me happy beyond belief."

Behind me, the patrons of the coffee shop erupted in applause.

I looked at Merriwether. "Thank you, thank you for this gift."

We all piled into her Honda and went back to my house. Cupcake and her crew were loitering as usual, but I didn't even notice them. My eyes were for Destiny and Destiny only.

Once settled inside, I popped open a bottle of champagne (and filled a glass with OJ for my baby) and toasted the grand occasion.

After a few sips, I turned to Merriwether and said, "Of course, I want to be completely involved in Destiny's life, and I'm willing to pay child support—even for the years I didn't know about her."

My eyes were welling up again.

"I would like shared custody as well," I said, smiling proudly over at Destiny.

Merriwether gave her mother a careful look before setting her champagne flute down onto the table and saying, "Well, about that, you see . . ."

Chevy

· · · · · · · · · · · ·

I spent Sunday and Monday night in the park. My mind, too busy for sleep, teemed with memories of my childhood, my teenage years, and my present-day life.

I looked down at my filthy clothes.

I was homeless; there was no doubt about that. I had to come to the realization. I had to finally accept the truth about my circumstances and my life up to this point.

Who was I to blame? Every time I tried to point the finger at someone or something else, I looked down at my finger and it was pointed right at me.

I sat down on a bench and cried my way through the night. When I finally stopped crying it was Tuesday morning and I was a new woman.

· · ·

The hallways were buzzing with La Fleur employees. I strolled as casually as possible toward my office, but my filthy appearance called attention to me.

When I reached my office, the door was slightly ajar. I eased it open and walked in to see LaTangie seated behind my desk.

"Can I help you?" I asked sternly.

"No, I think it's can I help *you*?" she replied with a smirk.

"Look, I don't have time for your games today, LaTangie, so get your ass out of my chair and the hell out of my office."

LaTangie let out a long wicked laugh and then pointed at the nameplate on the desk. It said LATANGIE FOX.

Reaching for the phone, LaTangie barked, "No, you get your ass out of *my* office before I call security!"

In a strange way I felt relieved. I looked around the office. I wanted to commit it to memory—it had been good while it lasted.

LaTangie gave me an awed look. "Are you really that stupid, Chevy?" Laughing, she pressed the button for security. "You don't work here anymore. You didn't show up for Anja's Memorial Day party, the most important event of the year. What were we supposed to do?"

We?

"We didn't know if you were alive or dead or working somewhere else," she said, chuckling. "Only God knows who would have you in their employ, since you're such a fuck-up!" she roared joyfully.

I guess she must have pushed a button I didn't know existed. Or maybe the weight and stress of the last week—shit, the last ten years—had finally caused me to crack, because before I could stop myself I was sailing over the desk.

I hit LaTangie head-on, and we both went toppling to the

floor. I punched her with a left, a right, and a left again before grabbing hold of her hair (which I'd known all the while was a weave—you can't play a player) and yanking with all my might until I'd virtually snatched her bald.

Then I jumped up and pulled the phone line from the wall. I knew she wasn't going to make a run for it—she was too busy blubbering and gathering her tracks, which were scattered all over the carpet.

"I hope your johns downtown like your new look!" I spat.

The look on LaTangie's face told me that it was her I saw in that seedy hotel.

I gave her one last pitiful look and walked out of the office. I was going to leave the building, but at the last minute I changed my mind. It wouldn't be right of me to leave without saying goodbye to Anja, now would it?

Crystal

· · · · · · · · · · · · ·

I couldn't believe my ears. "I—I don't understand, Noah."

Noah took a deep breath and started with "Remember that summer when I was sick?"

"Sick?"

"Sick, girl, sick—out of my fucking mind . . . the summer I spent sleeping with . . . yuck, women!"

"Oh, yeah, I remember," I said, and then it dawned on me. "I thought you were being safe, using condoms, I—"

"You know me better than that. Of course I was being safe. But things happen, you know."

Boy, did I!

"The condom broke, but I didn't know it, and so Merriwether got pregnant and—"

"Merriwether? A white girl?"

"No, she's a sister . . . Can you please stop interrupting me?"

"Sorry."

"So Merriwether turns up pregnant and she don't know where to find me, 'cause it was just a one-night stand—you know how I was doing . . ."

Yeah, I knew.

"But here's the kicker: she was engaged to an old lover of mine named Will Somers when she slept with me."

"Will Somers? One of your old lovers? Noah, I—I don't understand."

This story was getting weirder by the minute.

"Yes, Crystal—damn, don't act like you don't know about brothers playing on both teams.

"Any-hoo, I bumped into both of them in London . . . No one was more surprised than I was when I found out that he was marrying a female."

My head was spinning.

"But the marriage didn't even last. Will decided that he pre-ferred dick and had the marriage annulled."

"Are you serious?"

"Dead serious. Then Destiny was born."

"Destiny?"

"Destiny, that's her name, my daughter," Noah said, his voice swelling with pride.

I was trying hard to follow the story.

"I saw Will in the subway station when I was coming to Geneva's Christmas in May celebration, and he told me that Merriwether was looking for me and passed her number on to me." Noah exhaled long and hard and then said, "Which is how we come around to now."

I just blinked. This story was as unbelievable as they come.

"Damn, Noah."

"That's what I said, but there's more."

That was enough, I thought, but said, "Go on."

"Merriwether wants me to raise the child. She wants me to have sole custody."

"What?"

How could a woman give her child up? What kind of mother was she!

"You, why?"

Noah was quiet for a minute. I guess my tone had been hard and judging, because I believed a child needed a mother, especially a girl child.

Noah was a man, a gay man at that, I thought, and only right then and there did it make sense. I'm sure Noah was probably more woman than Merriwether was.

"Why not me?"

"No, no, Noah," I said, softening my tone. I had to clean this up, and fast. "I just wanted to know why it was a woman would want to give up her child?"

"Well," Noah began thoughtfully, "she loves her, of that I'm sure, but she's been unemployed for more than a year and living with her mother in a studio apartment in Crown Heights. And well, Crystal, she's sick."

"Sick?"

"She was diagnosed with MS and it's progressing rapidly. The doctors say that in six months she'll be bound to a wheelchair."

"Oh, shit, Noah. I'm sorry to hear that."

"Yeah, I was too. It's not like she's abandoning Destiny—"

"No, of course not, Noah—she's turning her over to her father," I said.

"Yes, that's exactly what she's doing. Turning her over to her father, to me."

We were quiet for a while, listening to each other breathe. And then Noah piped up: "So, Miss Girl, you have a bun in the oven. What's Neville saying about it? . . . It is Neville's, right?"

Geneva

....

"**a** re you calm?" Deeka asked.

"Yes."

"Sure, Ma?"

"Yes," I squeezed out a second time from between clenched teeth.

I was flat on my back on the kitchen floor; Deeka had secured my right arm and Eric my left.

Charlie's screams had died down to tearful whimpering.

"Okay now, if we let you up, are you going to behave?" My son spoke to me like I was his child. I felt the rage begin to bubble again.

"Yes."

Deeka's face was practically pressed against mine, and he stared intently into my eyes.

"Nah, wait a minute, Eric. Her pupils are really dilated. Something is definitely not right here."

Eric leaned over and peered at my eyes. I felt like a guinea pig.

"Get out of my face."

My voice was quivering; I could feel myself about to lose control again.

" 'Neva." Deeka spoke softly, calmly. "Have you been taking anything?"

I shook my head no.

"Are you sure, nothing?"

I shook my head no again.

"What about your magic beans, Mommy?" Charlie's small voice sailed over to us.

I was busted!

"What are you talking about, Charlie?" Eric asked, raised his head.

"Mommy takes magic beans, like 'Jack and the Beanstalk,' but her magic beans will make her shrink."

Charlie was speaking real fast.

Deeka and Eric gave me a quizzical look.

"Right, Mommy?"

Charlie was standing over me now, her Pooh Bear clutched in her arms, her eyes red and swollen from crying, perfect pug nose moist and red.

I looked up at my darling daughter and then over to my son and boyfriend and whispered, "The child is confused . . . delusional . . . a liar, just like her father."

Deeka and Eric exchanged shocked looks.

"Charlie, do you know where Mommy keeps her magic beans?"

"In her pocketbook."

"Go get them for me, okay, munchkin?"

Charlie nodded and scurried off.

Deeka planted sad eyes on me. " 'Neva . . . why?"

What did he know?

He had never been publicly humiliated by the "Jelly Belly" song.

Crystal

●●●●●●●●●●●●●●

When I hung up with Noah my first instinct was to call Geneva, but my hand just couldn't seem to bring itself to dial her number. She'd been acting so whacked out lately that I didn't know how she would take the news, and I really didn't need a negative reaction from her.

She was my best friend, and it pained me not to be able to share this wonderful news with her.

I called my mother instead.

"Ma?"

"Hey, Chrissy. How are you, darling?"

I don't know why, but the sound of my mother's voice burst the dam I had been struggling to maintain, and all the sorrow, frustration, and happiness spilled out of me in one long wail.

"Mommmmmmy!"

"Oh, baby girl, what's wrong?"

I was a sobbing mess, but Peyton Atkins held it together for both us. Her voice remained calm, her words soothing.

After about ten minutes, I was able to collect myself enough to speak.

"Mommy, I-I'm pregnant."

She was quiet for a long moment, no doubt trying to process the words I'd just spoken.

"A baby?"

"Yes, in January."

"My baby is having a baby?"

"Yes, Mommy."

Peyton let off a long whistle and then her voice came back, filled with sunshine and excitement. "My baby is having a baby. I'm going to be a grandmother!"

I imagined her doing some kind of happy dance in the middle of her bedroom or wherever she was in her house, and then she began to cry, which got me to crying again too.

Chevy

· · · · · · · · · · · ·

O kay, okay now, just go slow, real slow . . . that's it . . . that's it . . . You got it now, baby. Oh, oh, watch the teeth—this ain't no sausage, you know.

"Yeah, yeah, that's better, *reaaal* good. Take it all in now, take it all in . . . I know it's a lot, but you can do it . . . They don't call you Deep Throat for nothing, now do they?"

Anja is grossly slipping up, I thought as I stood watching from the doorway. Wasn't nothing wrong with a little office delight, but how could one forget to lock the friggin' door?

I'd been standing there for a minute, amazed at how freaky it was to see Andre's female persona, all femmed up in an Etro silk blouse and skirt set, stockings dangling from one ankle, with legs up in the air, spread eagle, big hands clutching the inner part of her thighs while her elbows pressed deep into the cushy armrests of the chair, supporting the weight of her muscular legs.

The chair was tilted recklessly back on its stem, and that along with Andre's big, black cock seeming to torpedo out from beneath the colorful silk of the fabric made the whole scene look ludicrous at best.

Myra from Accounting was on her knees; the pumps she wore were new—no scuff marks on the soles. I wish I could say the same about her ass, riddled with pimples and liver spots—I guess it'd seen better days.

I watched in awe as Myra opened her perfect little mouth and swallowed all nine inches of Andre's dick.

I stifled a laugh and pulled my Razr camera phone from my back pocket. I would capture this scene for posterity, or at least for a few future laughs.

When the cool air flowed through the open door and hit Anja's wet dick, her eyes flew open.

"What the fuck?" she screamed, and roughly pushed Myra away. "Close the goddamn door, Chevy!"

And I did, slowly, of course; Anja's angry screams had made their way out into the hallway, drawing the concerned and curious from their offices.

"Have you lost your goddamn mind!" Anja barked, jumping from her chair and pushing her skirt down all in one action.

Myra crawled frantically around the floor, gathering articles of clothing.

"So, it seems that La Fleur Industries is nothing more than your personal whorehouse," I said as I calmly rested my hand on the doorknob.

Anja's eyes bulged. "Just what are you thinking about doing, Chevy, huh?"

I smiled smugly.

"You do remember signing a confidentiality clause, don't you?"

I nodded my head yes.

"You know if you break that clause I will prosecute. You know that, don't you?"

Anja wasn't Anja anymore; Anja was Andre now, in full baritone voice.

I grinned. We were one and the same, weren't we?

Both pretending to be someone we weren't.

Both using people for our own selfish purposes.

"I know you will," I sighed as I slowly turned the doorknob. "Pull your pantyhose up," I said matter-of-factly.

Anja's face twisted with surprise, and then she hurriedly bent over and pulled her pantyhose up and into place.

I looked over at Myra, who was struggling to button her blouse. When she raised her eyes to meet mine, they were crossed, their gaze fixed intently on her nose.

I pulled the door open and the crowd that had gathered in the hallway peered in.

"Good morning!" I greeted their curious faces with a bright smile before making my way around them and down the hall.

My cell phone clutched tightly in my hand, I began to laugh and continued to do so all the way down in the elevator, through the lobby, and out the door.

I laughed down Sixth Avenue and I'm sure my laughter could be heard through the grates of the subway station as I waited patiently for the F train.

Geneva

· · · · · · · · · · · · · · · ·

I sat quietly and obediently on the sofa. Charlie was snuggled up against me; Eric sat in a folding chair across from me, staring down at his hands.

Deeka was on the phone with the poison control center, my bottle of Biothin clutched tightly in his hand.

"Thank you very much," he said, and then hung up the phone. He released a long sigh before walking over and standing in front of me.

"The people at Biothin said that some people have an extreme mental or behavioral psychotic reaction to . . ." He stopped speaking and brought the bottle up to his face. He strained to read the small print before carefully enunciating the word: "ech-no-lysia."

"Echno-what?" Eric said, looking up at him.

"It's some type of extract found in a plant in South America," Deeka said, sitting down heavily on the couch and looking at me.

"They also said that that information is always included in their package orders."

I avoided his eyes.

"Did you read the information, Geneva?"

Of course I'd read some of it, but not all.

I didn't respond.

"What did the people at the poison control center say?" Eric's voice quaked a bit with his question.

Deeka took a deep breath. "They basically said the same thing that the Biothin people said, and suggested that we take her to the hospital."

Noah

· · · · · · · · · · ·

I felt as nervous as a virgin about to get my first piece.

"Zahn?"

I didn't know what time it was in New Delhi, and I didn't care.

"Noah, is that you?"

At least he sounded happy to hear from me.

"Something has happened."

"Are you okay? What's wrong?"

He was concerned. He still loved me. Thank God.

"I've thought about the whole children thing, and I agree, we should have a child."

For a while the only noise between us was the pulsating waves of static.

"Really?" Zahn finally replied.

"Yes, and—and . . ."

I didn't know just how to say it.

"And I have the perfect little girl."

"What?"

"It's a long story, Zahn, but I just found out I have a daughter."

Zahn laughed. "Is this some type of joke?"

"No, no, it's not a joke. I'm serious."

Again, silence.

"Zahn?"

"I'm a little confused, Noah. What do you mean, you have a daughter?"

I looked at the clock. This was going to be a very expensive phone call.

It would be cheaper to have Zahn fly to New York for a face-to-face.

"How about this," I started in an unsure voice. "How about you fly here and meet her for yourself?"

Crystal

· · · · · · · · · · · · · ·

I didn't expect the reaction that I received from Neville. When I passed on the news he let out a scream that pierced my eardrums and then he said, "I knew it, I knew it!"

"You knew? How?"

"I just had this feeling, Crystal. The last night you were here and we made love, neither of us realized the condom had come off, and—"

"The condom came off? I thought it must have broken."

"No, when you got up to go to the bathroom, it was lying on the sheet."

"Why didn't you say anything?"

"I didn't want to alarm you."

"So those phone calls, when you were asking if I was okay— you sounded so concerned . . . You knew then?"

"I felt it somehow. It's hard to explain. But then when you didn't say anything, I thought I was wrong."

"This is so freaky."

"Yeah, it is."

"So you're happy about this? You don't mind if I have the baby?"

"Mind? Why would I mind you bringing my child—our child—into the world?"

"Your lifestyle . . ."

"Do you think that would interfere with me being a good father?"

"You're a good person, Neville. I suspect that means you would be a good father and a loving one."

"Crystal." Neville's voice became serious. "I would want to spend as much time with you and the baby as possible. You know that, right?"

Oh God—was he going to propose marriage?

"Yes, I know that."

"So, um—if you want to . . . me and you . . . the baby . . ."

My heart was bursting. I loved Neville: he was a good man, a good friend, and a wonderful lover. But I knew the one thing he wouldn't be good at was being a husband.

"Are you trying to ask me to marry you, Neville?"

He let out a small laugh. "I guess I was."

"I don't need that, Neville. I need a friend and a father for this child. That's what I need."

Neville sighed. "That's what you got, Crystal."

Chevy

• • • • • • • • • • • • •

just as I stepped off the F train at Jay Street Borough Hall, the A train pulled into the station.

The other passengers and I hurried onto the train and scrambled for seats.

I was going to Brooklyn, going to Noah's, going back home. I felt like I was climbing out of a bad dream that had been going on for most of my adult life. It felt good to finally wake up.

I stretched my legs out, put my head back, and closed my eyes.

"Spare some change, miss?"

I parted my eyelids. In front of me stood a woman. Her lips were bloated, her eyes red, her clothes grimy and tattered.

She held a filthy palm under my nose.

"Change?" she said again when I opened my eyes the whole way.

I didn't have much, but the few dollars I did have I pressed into her palm.

The block was quiet except for a few young adults hanging out on the stoop next door to Noah's house.

They gave me an odd look and then whispered behind their palms.

Climbing the stairs to the front door, I began to feel a bit nervous. My hands were shaking when I tried to fit the key into the lock.

"Damn, he changed the locks," I murmured to myself.

I straightened my shoulders, smoothed my hair back into place, and held my head high as I brought my finger up and pressed the bell.

Crystal

· · · · · · · · · · · · · ·

Kendrick called. To tell you the truth, I'd forgotten all about him.

"Hey, Crystal. I'm just calling to see if you're feeling better?"

"I'm feeling fine—thanks for asking, Kendrick."

I sounded so formal. This wasn't going to be easy.

"Um, well . . . can I come by and see you?"

I took a deep breath and exhaled loudly before I began.

"Kendrick, you're a really good guy. You've pulled yourself together, and—"

"Are you breaking up with me?"

"C'mon, Kendrick, were we really officially back together?"

"Crystal, we—we made love. Didn't that mean anything to you?"

"It did. It meant the world to me, and I thank you for sharing yourself with—"

"You *thank* me? What's going on with you . . . ? We talked about our futures."

"That's before I knew I was pregnant, Kendrick."

The line went dead silent.

"You're pregnant?"

"Yeah, two months."

"Wow. I guess congratulations are in order."

"Thank you, Kendrick."

"Crystal?"

"Yes?"

"Do you love him . . . the father?"

"I love him in a way that I don't think you can understand, because I don't even understand it."

"That's deep."

"Yeah, it is."

"So, um, hey—don't be a stranger, okay?"

"Of course not. There's someone out there for you, Kendrick."

"Yeah, there is, but she just told me she's pregnant with another man's child."

A soft click followed those last words, and then a blaring dial tone.

Geneva

·················

I spent five days in detox at New York Hospital.

I don't remember most of what went on with me while I was on the Biothin. But from the stories I've heard, I'm not very proud of myself.

My nurses thought I was some kind of celebrity because of all the flowers I received. Deeka and Eric alone filled up that room like the botanical gardens.

Eric brought flowers for me every day, and Deeka, well, he just had them delivered on a daily basis because he never left my side.

When Crystal came to visit me, she was glowing, and I knew before she even told me that she was expecting. We held each other and cried. I apologized for whatever it was I said and did to her while I was under the influence.

She told me that apologies weren't necessary; all I needed to do was agree to be the godmother of her child. I told her that nothing but death would keep me from it.

I almost didn't know Chevy when she walked in the door. She looked thinner, and that edge she'd always had about her was gone. She was all soft curves now.

I'd heard from Crystal that she'd been through some stuff, most of which she wasn't ready to talk about, and I didn't press her. I just wrapped my arms around her and hugged tight.

When she told me that I looked good, I knew for sure a new day had dawned. Chevy never, ever paid me a compliment, not in all the years we'd known each other.

I said, "You look good too, girl." And Chevy actually blushed!

Noah followed not too much later, Zahn by his side, and both carried large brown shopping bags. They were grinning like Cheshire cats. I figured whatever news they had must be huge.

My eyes swung to Crystal, then Chevy, but they all averted their eyes. No one was going to give me a hint.

"What's going on?"

How the hospital had allowed it, I don't know—all the people in that room must have had some sort of influence over somebody—but in walked two little girls. One of which was my daughter Charlie.

The other one, I thought I knew, because her face seemed so familiar to me.

"Hey, baby," I called to my daughter. "Who's your friend?"

"This is Destiny," Charlie said. "Destiny, this is my mommy."

Destiny waved shyly at me.

I looked at Noah, who looked as if he was going to burst.

"Okay, I give. Who is—" I started to speak and then stopped. It was like I'd been struck.

"Oh, shit!" I yelled, and popped straight up in my hospital bed.

"That's a potty word, Mommy!" Charlie yelled.

"S-sorry, baby," I said, my eyes swinging between Destiny and Noah.

"Is this—"

I couldn't even get the words out of my mouth before Noah yelled, "My daughter!" and then he glanced at Zahn and said, "Our daughter."

Someone could have knocked me over with a feather.

I called both little ones to me, pulled them up onto the bed, and covered their tiny, beautiful faces with kisses.

"Gosh," I sighed, looking around at all my friends, "our family just keeps growing, doesn't it?"

Everybody nodded in agreement.

"I don't know how much more news I could take," I said, pressing my hand against my heart.

"Well," Crystal started, coming to sit on the bed, "I've decided that I'm going to move."

That made sense; she always had a love for the country. She was probably going up to Westchester . . . That wasn't too far. I could catch Metro-North up to see her.

"Where?"

"Antigua."

I just blinked.

"Antigua?"

"I've had a enough of New York, Geneva. I hate my job, I hate the crime and the dirt . . . I don't want to raise my child here. I want him or her to be able to breathe fresh air, eat fresh fruit, and swim in the ocean all year round. I want Neville and me to raise our child together."

I will not cry. I will not cry.

"Sure, sure, I understand," I said, forcing myself to sound happy.

"That's wonderful, Crystal girl," Noah said. "Destiny can come and spend the summers with you!"

"Sure, she can," Crystal said, giving the little girl a quick tweak on her nose. "Antigua is a popular vacation spot for the British."

I looked at Noah and asked, "You're going back to England?"

Noah sighed. "Yes, that's were Zahn's work is, Geneva."

I looked over at Chevy, who had been the quietest I'd ever seen her.

"And you, Chevy, where are you going?"

Chevy smiled. "I'm going to my mother's."

"In Pittsburgh!" we all said in unison.

"Girl, you must have had a session with Jesus himself. I can't imagine you in Pittsburgh!" Noah laughed and he and Crystal did a high-five.

"I know. It may just be for a little while. I don't know . . . I have some things to sort out."

"Good for you," I said, and then, "Well, is that it? Is there more?" I looked around at the faces looking back at me.

Deeka stepped through. His expression was as serious as I'd ever seen it. My body began to shake, and I just knew this man was going to announce right in front of all my friends that he was leaving me.

" 'Neva."

"Y-yes, Deeka."

Well, I'd put him through a lot, hadn't I? He was a young man and probably didn't expect all this drama from a mature woman like myself. I wouldn't try to stop him if he wanted to go.

I would wish him well and just be happy for the year we had together. I would handle this like a real woman should.

"I love you with all of my being. I've loved you from the first time I walked into the diner and laid eyes on you. I have never ever felt this way about any other woman that's been in my life—that's how I know that what I feel for you is real.

"I wanted to take you somewhere romantic and propose marriage to you, but here and now with all of your friends—I mean our friends—seems more than perfect for a time and place."

The tears were spilling from my eyes so fast that my entire face was wet.

"I want to ask you, the love of my heart, my best friend, my lover, if you will also be my wife?"

And with those final words, Deeka took my hand and slipped the most beautiful ring I'd ever seen onto my finger.

Noah leaned over, made an approving sound in his throat, and then said, "Yellow sapphires and diamonds—man, you got taste!"

I hadn't answered. I was too busy crying and kissing my man.

"Answer him, Mommy, answer him!"

"Yes, yes, yes!"

December

Chevy

. . . .

I decided that Pittsburgh really wasn't all that bad. It wasn't New York, but that was okay.

I took a job working alongside my mother at her hair salon. It's harder than it looks—I'm on my feet for twelve, sometimes fourteen hours, and not every customer is a dream to work with, if you know what I mean.

But at the end of the day, it's an honest living and an honest dollar—not as much as I'm used to making, but enough to keep me humble.

I'm staying with my mother and am in no hurry to move. She's teaching me how to cook and sew and knit—if you can believe it. And I'm getting pretty good at all three.

My time away from her made me forget just how much I need her in my life.

She's a pretty hip chick, to tell you the truth, and we've been having a ball hanging out together.

I'm seeing somebody too.

His name is Chet and he's a mechanic. Okay, "mechanic" is a bit of a stretch—he's a gas station attendant.

I know—who would have thought it—Chevanese Cambridge dating a gas station attendant?

Hey, people change.

We're all going down to Geneva and Deeka's wedding—and you want another shocker? I bought Chet's ticket!

What happened to Anja?

Well, Anja is no more.

Someone started circulating on the Internet a picture taken of her in a compromising position.

I read in the paper that when she left work one day, a crowd was waiting for her, shouting: "Show us your dick!"

After weeks of denying that she was in fact a man, Anja finally came out of the closet—so to speak—and admitted it.

What followed was more humiliating than having his cover blown. Someone dropped a serious dime that La Fleur Industries was not only the parent company to Anja's popular media organization but the front for Freaks R Us escort service.

Anja, aka Andre, had been the head pimp/madam in charge!

The feds swooped in and shut down the entire operation. Last time I heard, La Fleur Industries' stock had plummeted from sixty-five dollars a share down to a buck and a quarter!

And Anja, aka Andre, was out on a $300,000 bail, awaiting trial.

Noah

• • • • • • • • • •

destiny adapted real well to the preschool here. She's as
smart as a whip, and every day she makes me proud.

Zahn is as much in love with her as I am. We've already
started looking for a house—the toys and stuffed animals we've
bought for her need their own zip code!

I send money to Merriwether every month, and we bought
her a computer, complete with a videoconference camera so that
she and Destiny can see and speak to each other anytime they
want.

I sold my house and walked away with a very tidy little sum
of money. I was able to start Destiny's trust fund and put some
down on one of those new condo apartments they've built in
Bed-Stuy.

What, did you think I was never coming back?

What are you, crazy? I love New York and simply adore Brooklyn!

I heard through the grapevine that one morning a dozen undercover cops showed up at Cupcake's front door, warrant in hand, and found a shitload of cocaine in her basement.

I wonder if she'll be roasting a hog on cellblock C?

Crystal

· · · · · · · · · · · · ·

I sublet my apartment but cleaned out my 401(k).

I bought the most adorable house in Antigua. It has three bedrooms and two bathrooms and an ocean view, and best of all, it's right down the road from Neville.

Our son, Javid, was born on December 20, one month ahead of schedule.

He is perfect. I can't imagine that I lived all those years without him.

Neville is the proudest papa I've ever known—not counting Noah, of course. Javid and I see him twice a day, and sometimes he even spends the night.

I'm not working, but I have been thinking about starting my own little business down here.

Wedding planning.

I so enjoyed helping Geneva plan her wedding, and Noah said when he and Zahn agree on the date for their commitment ceremony he wants me to do the same for him.

Here Comes the Bride!

Geneva

· · · · · · · · · · · · · · · · ·

When Crystal suggested that I get married in Antigua, I was all for it and agreed that we would before I'd even discussed it with Deeka.

Thank God he loved the idea.

Now here I stand, my first plane ride under my belt, my gorgeous son at my side, Charlie and Destiny floating ahead of me, dropping hibiscus petals along the carpet of sea grass that's stretched out before me and across the sand.

Yes, a beach wedding, and at sunset, no less!

The steel band begins to play the wedding march and I hear my mother, Doris B., begin to cry.

"You ready, Mom?" Eric asks.

"I think I finally am," I say, and link my arm with his.

I move as if in a dream. My bridesmaids, Chevy and Noah— yes, Noah—smile at me as I float by them.

Crystal, my maid of honor, kisses me lovingly on my cheek, her own cheeks wet with tears, as I hand her my bouquet.

I turn to face my lover, my friend, my soul mate, and future. Our hands lock and we gaze lovingly into each other's eyes as the minister begins . . .

"Do you, Geneva Lillian Holliday, take this man to be your lawfully wedded husband . . . ?"

You're still reading, so you must be looking for more.

You're smart; you know that it's not really over until the fat lady sings. So let me steal a line from that soulful group the Delfonics to let you know just how much I appreciate you.

(throat clearing)

Here goes:

"La, la, la, la, la, la, la, la, laaaa, la, means I love you . . ."

Gratitude . . .

This has been such a fun ride!

I am most grateful to the universe, my wonderful editor Phyllis Grann, and my equally fabulous publicist Laura Pillar, as well as everyone at Broadway Books who worked so hard to make the Groove series a success.

A big thank-you to my family, friends, readers, fellow authors, and book clubs—all of whom continue to support me on so many different levels. Many thanks to my #1 fan in St. Louis, Evan Hilliard—who has shown me nothing but love from day one!

And last but far from least—thank you to my beautiful daughter, R'yane Azsa, who continues to make me proud.

Good things,

Geneva